CR
2
A
Fully e

Crocodi
**Centre and Rescue Response Unit is home to a
team of expertly trained medical professionals.
These dedicated men and women face the
challenges of life, love and medicine every day!**

Two weddings!
Crocodile Creek is playing host to two weddings
this year, and love is definitely in the air! But…

A cyclone is brewing!
As a severe weather front moves in,
the rescue team are poised for action—
this time with some new recruits.

Two missing children!
As the cyclone wreaks its devastation, it soon
becomes clear that there are two little ones missing.
Now the team has to pull together like never before
to find them…before it's too late!

Dear Reader

Our starting point for this second *Crocodile Creek* mini-series was 'a cyclone and weddings', and the whole thing dropped into place with amazing speed when we talked about it together. Something to do with our friendship as writers. The ideas sparked between us and we had no disagreements about how these books should develop.

Something to do with that whole idea of human celebration in the face of nature's devastation, too. People just seem to have an innate need to seek renewal and emotional connection even while the storm is still raging, and that balance of loss and renewal seemed so right in these books.

Some of you may not know this, but cyclones and hurricanes are really the same thing—they just spin in opposite directions—so if you're wondering just how intense our Cyclone Willie was, think of some of the most infamous hurricanes, only in a region of scattered population, tropical farms and rugged rainforest. Some of the devastation we describe comes from eye-witness accounts of Cyclone Larry, a powerfully destructive storm which hit the coast of far north Queensland in March 2006.

But of course it's the positive things we like to focus on as romance writers. There's more than one happy ending in this book…

All the best

Lilian Darcy

LONG-LOST SON: BRAND-NEW FAMILY

BY
LILIAN DARCY

MILLS & BOON
Pure reading pleasure

First published in Great Britain 2007
Harlequin Mills & Boon Limited,
Eton House, 18-24 Paradise Road, Richmond, Surrey TW9 1SR

© Lilian Darch 2007

ISBN: 978 0 263 85279 0

Set in Times Roman 10½ on 12¼ pt
03-1207-49341

Printed and bound in Spain
by Litografia Rosés, S.A., Barcelona

Lilian Darcy is Australian, but has strong ties to the USA through her American husband. They have four growing children, and currently live in Canberra, Australia. Lilian has written over seventy romance novels, and still has more story ideas crowding into her head than she knows what to do with. Her work has appeared on romance bestseller lists, and two of her plays have been nominated for major Australian writing awards. 'I'll keep writing as long as people keep reading my books,' she says. 'It's all I've ever wanted to do, and I love it.' Find out more about Lilian and her books at her website, www.liliandarcy.com, or write to her at PO Box 532, Jamison PO, Macquarie, ACT 2614, Australia.

Recent titles by the same author:

PREGNANT WITH HIS CHILD (*Crocodile Creek*)
THE LIFE-SAVER
THE DOCTOR'S FIRE RESCUE

**Did you know that Lilian
also writes for Mills & Boon® Special Edition™?
A few of her recent titles include:**

THE COUPLE MOST LIKELY TO
OUTBACK BABY
PRINCESS IN DUSGUISE

PROLOGUE

FELIXX had fallen asleep now, thank goodness. He looked uncomfortable, with his cheek pressed against the sill below the darkened, rain-splashed window of the bus. Janey's heart hurt when she looked at him. He was only five years old, and he hadn't spoken a word to her. Not in the two hours they'd been on the bus, or over the past three days since she'd arrived at Mundarri. He hadn't spoken a word to anyone, and no one could tell her why.

Was she doing the right thing?

As soon as news had reached her about Alice's death, she'd taken indefinite leave from her group general practice in Darwin. Had managed to reach Mundarri via a roundabout route of hops by air in frighteningly small planes, and finally a lift from one of Mundarri's other residents, a woman named Maharia.

Everyone at Mundarri seemed to have chosen odd names for themselves. Janey gathered this was part of the philosophy of the place—that you gave yourself a fresh start with a new and more spiritual name. Alice had become Alanya, although Janey could never think of her by that name. Little Felixx had originally been named Francis James, which his dad had soon shortened to Frankie Jay, she remembered.

Anyway… The Mundarri people had all seemed nice enough. Caring. Very gentle and warm with Felixx, as Janey was learning to call him.

And yet they let my sister die.

Yes, OK, so she was a doctor, trained within what the Mundarri people regarded as the uncompromising scientific straitjacket of Western medicine, but the fact was Alice's liver had packed up and a 'cleansing diet' of carrot juice was just never going to cut it in the healing department.

Alice had needed urgent hospital treatment, and probably a transplant down the track, and the people at Mundarri, out of arrogance or naivety or goodness knows what, hadn't called an ambulance for her until it had been far too late.

Thinking about it, Janey found she was crying. Anger and grief and doubt all mixed up together.

Had she done the right thing?

Felixx could have stayed at Mundarri. It would have taken some lengthy wrangling with the authorities, but one of the women—Maharia, or who was that other one Felixx had seemed close to? Raina?—could have been named his legal guardian and he would have continued to live in a place that was at least familiar.

A place whose irresponsible, ill-informed healing philosophies had killed his mother.

No, she had done the right thing, taking him away.

But she didn't know what she was going to do next, because it turned out Felixx had a father living just a few hours from here, and Janey had had no idea. It had been a huge shock to discover Luke Bresciano's contact details among Alice's things, and to discover that Crocodile Creek was, by Australian standards, so close.

Beyond the confines of the bus, night had fallen completely now. The sodden blanket of cloud overhead let no moonlight through, and the rain was relentless, noisy and thick and buffeted by wind. There was a cyclone hovering out to sea, apparently, and people were saying it was getting closer and stronger, and might hit the coast. In these conditions, you could easily believe it.

The bus rounded a bend and Felixx slid toward Janey, still fast asleep. She pillowed his head on her shoulder and wondered yet again why he wouldn't speak.

It wasn't a defiant silence, she thought. It came from…fear?

Or grief. He'd just lost his mother.

Oh, lord, could she herself possibly give him what he needed? At thirty-four, she'd never had a child. She loved him, but she didn't know him, because she and Alice had lived so far from each other since he was born, and Alice had made so little effort to keep in touch. 'I can't deal with cities any more,' she'd said. 'I need the wilderness.'

Luke Bresciano was Felixx's father. Janey needed to at least consider the possibility that he might want his son, despite everything Alice had said to the contrary. And she had to consider that Luke might be the best person to have him.

Was she doing the right thing?

Felixx felt warm against her side, and it was getting rather steamy in the damp bus. They rounded another bend and the bus skidded suddenly, bringing forth a chorus of alarmed gasps and cries.

'Sorry, folks,' the driver called. 'It's evil out there.'

How much longer till they reached the coast? They were late, surely. Should have been there by now. Janey had counted on arriving in time to organise motel accommodation for tonight—this whole trip hadn't even been on her agenda this time yesterday. She couldn't just show up on Luke Bresciano's doorstep without warning.

Stay asleep, little man, so at least you're fresh when we get there…

She put her arm around his little shoulder, thinking that he seemed so small for his age, loved but possibly not as well nourished as he should have been. They were strict vegans at Mundarri, there wasn't a lot of money on hand for fancy nutritional supplements, and it took a great deal of commitment to provide adequate nutrition for a child's growing body on that kind of diet.

His clothing, too… There was a hole in his sneaker that someone—Alice?—had tried to disguise with a cheerful picture of an orange clownfish. And there were mosquito bites, fresh ones and old ones, all over his skin. Alice's rainforest paradise had had its downside.

Where was the best place for this little boy? Should Janey have taken him back to Darwin with her and contacted Luke later on? But she didn't want Felixx's future hanging in limbo for months on end.

Her heart hurt again. What was the best thing for this precious waif of a child?

And then, right in the middle of the wash of churning emotion, the bus gave a tremendous, unexpected lurch. There was no more room for thought. A wild lashing of rain and wind slammed into the vehicle's side and it began to lean and slide. Outside, there came a violent, unearthly roaring sound. The bus driver yelled and swore. Couldn't he get the steering back under control? Come on... Come on...

Janey tried to keep hold of Felixx with one hand while fending them both off the seat-back in front with the other. The bus slid and heaved. She screamed. Chaos erupted, and then blackness.

CHAPTER ONE

'WHO do we still have left?' Luke asked wearily, craning his head for a quick look through the half-open door of the back room at the Bellambour Post Office and General Store.

'Only three,' Nurse Marcia Flynn promised. 'Want to see the kid next? He's ten, he's doing pretty well, but I think that arm is broken.'

'Displaced?'

'Not that I could see. I'm just going on how much it's hurting him.'

'Normally, I'd tell the parents to take him into Crocodile Creek and get it X-rayed,' Luke said. He was an orthopaedic surgeon, he didn't believe in letting bones heal crooked.

But conditions were far from normal in the wake of Cyclone Willie, as they all knew. Even supposing the ten-year-old's parents still had an operational vehicle, which some people didn't, the roads were a mess, and southbound traffic ran in a slow, continuous stream as people evacuated the cyclone-ravaged coast of Far North Queensland. The hospital was running around the clock, as Luke himself had been doing for three days, living on snatched sleep and even sketchier meals.

He'd only made it back to the doctors' house for the occasional change of underwear. He'd even showered and slept at the hospital, and had attempted to tune out the mess of stories and rumours that swirled in the cyclone's wake. Out of stubbornness, or something else?

Grace O'Riordan was in the ICU while Harry Blake looked like death warmed up, Georgie Turner had been swept off her feet by that visiting American neurosurgeon, Alistair, while the two of them had been rescuing Georgie's seven-year-old stepbrother, a dog and another kid from the very jaws of the storm.

The kid.

Luke was a self-destructive idiot for even thinking about the kid...

Now, here he was in the post office of this little town an hour north of Crocodile Creek at what the local State Emergency Service had turned into a makeshift medical clinic. So that the citizens of Bellambour who weren't planning to leave the town could see a doctor if they needed to.

Charles Wetherby had virtually ordered Luke to take some time off that morning. 'You made it to Mike and Emily's wedding celebration for, what, twenty minutes, the other night?' Crocodile Creek Hospital's medical director had accused. 'Just long enough to get Alistair Carmichael's blood up when you danced with Georgie. And you've been working nonstop since. You need to get out of this place and breathe some air.'

'I'm fine, Charles.' Gritted teeth.

'You're not, but I can tell you don't want to talk about it.'

'I don't want any time off.' Not until Janey Stafford had regained consciousness and he would hopefully be able to see her. Until then, he'd take any distractions he could.

And he wouldn't think about the kid.

'Would it help if I sent you on a busman's holiday?' Charles had asked.

'If you'll tell me what that is.'

'Hmm, I keep forgetting that anyone under thirty-five only learns American slang. I'll send you out on a clinic run, so you can at least have a change of scene while you work yourself into the ground. That's what I'm trying to say.'

'That'd be great…' he'd said, meaning it.

'Check the broken arm out the old-fashioned way, by feel,' Marcia said now.

'And then a backslab and a bandage,' Luke agreed, dragging his focus back. 'Shouldn't be a tough case. If it is displaced, I'll cross that bridge when I come to it.'

'If it's not washed away, like half the other bridges around here.'

He gave a dutiful laugh. It came out rusty, so different from the charm-laden sound he'd once used to such good effect. He sighed. 'OK, I'll see him next.'

'And then the old man, and last of all you can get to the guy who's doing all the complaining!'

'You're punishing him for complaining the most?'

'I think if there was really something wrong with him, he wouldn't have the energy left for it.'

'The Flynn triage system.' He appreciated Marcia. She was quick-witted and cheerful, the type who used nursing as a ticket to see the world, and good for her, having that spirit of adventure. He liked a woman with energy and spark. She probably wouldn't stay in

Crocodile Creek much longer. 'Treat the quiet ones first. I like it, Marcia.'

But his heart wasn't really committed to the conversation, Luke knew. He'd been like this for three days, running on autopilot, locking back into focus when he saw a serious case but at other times not really *there*. When he looked back on the incredible days of the cyclone and its aftermath in the weeks and months to come, he knew he would probably remember it differently to how everyone else did.

Because of Janey Stafford.

Three days ago in the middle of the night, just hours before the cyclone had hit, hearing Janey's name in the A and E department when Marcia had turned up some ID, he'd felt an electric prickle of shock all the way up his spine. He'd had to check the woman's identity for himself, with his own eyes—reach out and take a look beneath her oxygen mask to make sure it was really and seriously the same Janey Stafford, Alice's sister, not someone else.

He'd recognised her at once. The glossy mid-brown hair, the brown eyes, the freckles, the features that weren't quite regular enough to make her beautiful, except when she smiled, which of course she hadn't been doing then, in her unconscious state.

And although he'd played down their past relationship to his colleagues, he'd been thinking about her ever since. Wondering why she was there. Wondering if he was kidding himself that it had anything to do with him. Remembering how steady and sensible she'd always been, unlikely to come to Crocodile Creek on a whim. Thinking of his lost son and—

Stop it, Luke.

You can't afford this.

The ten-year-old with the iffy arm appeared in the makeshift clinic along with his mum, and Luke snapped back into the pretence of focus—into the cheerful humour that his fellow doctors might think was designed to lighten the atmosphere of disaster and loss all around them, but they were wrong. The humour was really just a way of anchoring himself to the work he had to do.

'So?' he said to the scruffy ten-year-old. 'Circus tricks? Rodeo riding? Jumping off a fence wearing paper wings and trying to fly?'

The kid gave a reluctant grin. 'Nah. We were cleaning up the mud in the living room and I slipped on it.' Not a story you were tempted to doubt when he still had a crust of dried mud all down his side, and when dozens of homes around here had fine, flood-washed silt inches thick on their floors. The mother nodded, too.

'You didn't consider a bath before you came in?'

'We're saving water.'

Ironic, when they'd just had about twenty inches of the stuff coming down from the sky, but Luke understood the situation. The family could have lost their rainwater tank in the storm, creeks were contaminated with debris and dead animals, town mains supplies were cut off or compromised in some other way. The damage and danger hadn't ended on Sunday with the passage of the storm.

'How's your arm now? Does it hurt?' He went through some standard questions and checks, decided the forearm was fractured but not displaced and so the backslab and bandage would be fine. He'd do it himself because Marcia was still treating some dodgy-looking cuts on their previous patient.

And while he wrapped the bandage, he wondered about Janey.

If she'd been brought out of her medically induced coma.

If she was talking yet.

If she was in contact with her sister.

If he could possibly go and sit beside her hospital bed and wangle anything out of her about Frankie Jay. If she acted cagey, told out-and-out lies, or if she really knew nothing, the way she'd claimed the last time he'd spoken to her by phone from England several years ago.

'Just a couple of mosquito bites.'

He blinked. The kid with the arm had gone, and here was the old man, playing down the infected bites covering a pair of ancient, skinny, reddish-purple legs which didn't look as if they boasted very good circulation.

And, of course, Luke was aware that he'd finished with the kid and called the old man in.

Of course he was.

He'd said the right words. *Bring him in to the hospital outpatient department in two weeks, Mum, so we can check that arm. Good luck with the mud. Tell me what I can do for you today, Mr Connolly.* But once again he'd been operating on autopilot the whole time.

'Bit nasty, though, aren't they?' he said about the bites. 'Have you been wading around in some of this water?'

The old man shrugged. 'Helping my son on the farm. Crop's destroyed. Take us years to get on our feet again. Never seen anything like that rain.'

'Wish we could send some of it to the drought areas down south, hey?' Luke took a closer look at the bites and decided that a topical cream wouldn't be enough to combat the multiple sites of infection, some of which were crusted with yellow-white pus. The man needed a course of oral antibiotic, but would he remember to take it? He'd probably rely on his daughter-in-law or his son to remind him. The man's skin felt warm to the touch. 'Pretty sticky out there, is it?'

Another shrug. 'Not too bad.'

Luke wrote out the script, gave some instructions and saw the old man's eyes glaze over. 'Show the tablets to your daughter-in-law,' he said firmly. 'She'll make sure you take them at the right times of day.'

'She's good,' Mr Connolly agreed. He hunched his shoulders, put a fist over his mouth and geared up for a cough, but nothing came. His breath wheezed in and out.

'Nothing else bothering you today, Mr Connolly?'

Something you're not talking about, the way I'm not talking about Janey, or the kid...

The man shook his head. 'It was me daughter-in-law brought me in, said I had to do something about the bites. I told her it was nothin' but she wouldn't listen.'

'She did the right thing.'

Marcia was mouthing something at Luke from the door with a frown on her face, and he had another one of those chills down his spine as an odd intuition kicked into high gear. He ushered the old man out, patting him on the back in an attempt to coax him to move faster. What did Marcia have to report?

'Someone's been asking for you,' she said, as soon as they were alone. 'That woman from the bus crash.'

'Janey Stafford,' he supplied automatically.

She raised her eyebrows. 'So you do know her.'

'I said I did, the other night.'

'You said you knew her sister.'

He wasn't going to respond to that. 'So she's conscious?' His head felt suddenly light, and his ears were ringing.

'Doing a lot better. They're talking about discharge tomorrow. She wants to see you, and—' She stopped suddenly.

'Yeah? What?' he growled, ill at ease.

'Nothing. One more patient. Roads are still crawling, apparently, people are just pouring out of the area and heading south, which is good because it means less stress on services. Did you take Mr Connolly's temperature?'

Luke went still. 'You asked me to, didn't you?' Damn, he'd totally forgotten, even when he'd touched the man's warm skin.

'I thought he was brewing a low-grade fever.'

'Has he left? Could you try and catch him? I completely forgot.'

Oh, hell, he didn't usually do this! He could have blamed the lack of sleep since Saturday, the stress, the makeshift conditions of the clinic, but he knew the problem was in his own head, and the distractions were far more personal, deeply rooted in his past. If Janey Stafford had come to Crocodile Creek because of him... If she had news about his son... If that unidentified kid whom Georgie and Alistair had found...

'So you think—?' Marcia began.

'I don't know what I think. What did you think?'

'I wondered about pneumonia. He's a smoker. I should have been more specific, Luke. I'm sorry, it's my fault as much as yours.'

'No, it isn't,' he retorted grimly. 'Just see if you can catch him. I should have given him a more thorough check.'

But Mr Connolly and his daughter-in-law had

already gone, and although Marcia tried to reach them by phone, there were so many equipment problems at the moment—lines down, towers damaged—she had no success. Luke made a mental note to himself to keep trying once they got back to Crocodile Creek.

'I cannot believe this,' Marcia said for about the fifth time, as they drove back. 'I just cannot believe this is the same landscape I drove through four weeks ago.'

She'd had a couple of days off back then, apparently, and had gone north for a bit of a wild beach weekend with a couple of female friends. Luke hadn't been up this way as recently, and didn't feel the need to express his reaction out loud—he'd learned to keep his emotions to himself in recent years—but he was just as shocked as Marcia, and no less so because they'd passed the same sights only that morning, on their way up. Seeing them in the other direction brought a fresh wave of disbelief.

There was such a dramatic grandeur about the huge mountains that backed this part of the coast, and with the region's bountiful rainfall they were always incredibly lush and green. Not any more. The rainforest's entire canopy had been shredded, leaving only straggly sticks. The twisted trunks and branches had even been scoured of their bark, as if sandblasted. It would take the landscape years to recover.

There were massive, beautiful trees, once lush with enormous canopies and huge branches hung thickly with epiphytes, but now reduced to trunks with a couple of stick-like branches poking up, their greenery lying in a shredded mulch on the ground and already beginning to rot.

Close by the highway, huge weeping figs lay one

after another on the ground, their root systems exposed, as if a giant hand had been pulling roadside weeds. Telephone poles leaned drunkenly, with their wires trailing in muddy pools.

They passed a house set back about fifty metres from the road—a typical old-fashioned Queenslander up on wooden pylons ten feet from the ground. Its front veranda and wall had been torn off and lay in a crumpled heap nearby, while its neat interior was open to display like a doll's house.

And the crops. Totally flattened. Sugar cane, bananas, pawpaws, with the farmers' ruined houses set in the middle of the destruction.

'What about the animals?' Marcia whispered again. 'The birds…'

'I know,' muttered Luke. Cassowaries, sugar gliders, tree frogs, possums, parrots, tree kangaroos, paddymelons, pythons, butterflies… The list went on, endangered species and common ones, predators and prey. Where would they find food and shelter now? 'But it's the people we have to think about.'

He slowed to a crawl behind an evacuating family in a loaded down minivan towing a trailer piled high with their belongings and covered with a badly tethered blue plastic tarpaulin. They probably had relatives somewhere down south, who'd promised to put them up until they could get back on their feet, make some decisions, sort out their finances.

'People help each other,' Marcia pointed out. 'Animals can't.'

'Nature is cruel,' Luke answered, sounding cruel himself, although he didn't mean to be. 'Marce, we're all pretty much in shock. Close your eyes and get some rest while we drive. Don't let it get to you so much, when we're so strapped as it is.'

'Oh, put up a few nice defensive walls?' She smiled to soften the statement.

'What's wrong with walls?' he said.

He knew what she must be thinking—that he must know all about walls. He hadn't asked any of the right questions about Janey Stafford. But he couldn't risk giving anything away. He couldn't bear to. His absurdly leaping hopes, all the anger and distrust, those irritating memories he still had of the time eight years ago when he and Janey had been colleagues.

She'd disapproved of him, and she'd let it show, even before he and her sister had fallen so wildly in love. She'd thought he was a lightweight, and that he relied on charm and networking to get what he wanted. In hindsight, there could have been some truth in all of that. He'd led a pretty charmed life until he'd married Alice Stafford.

Now Janey was asking for him. Which surely meant she must have come to Crocodile Creek to see him. And why would she have done that, unless…?

The shoe tortured him.

The stupid little shoe that Susie Jackson's sister Hannah had taken on as a personal quest, since arriving from New Zealand for Mike and Emily's wedding and getting caught up in the drama of the cyclone.

Who did the shoe belong to? What age of child would it fit? There had been two children missing following the bus crash up in the rainforest, they now knew—Georgie's little half-brother Max, aged seven, whom she hoped would be living with her permanently from now on, and the other boy that Georgie and Alistair had rescued from their hiding place in an old gold-mining shaft, whom Luke hadn't yet seen. The one who didn't speak, so they didn't even know his age or his name.

He knew Susie pretty well after his five months in Crocodile Creek, as a hospital physiotherapist and an orthopaedic surgeon tended to have a fair bit to do with each other professionally. She and Hannah were twins. Identical.

And there had been something quite disturbing about all this concern for a child's forlorn shoe coming from someone who wasn't Susie Jackson but who looked exactly like her. He'd had to hold himself back, pretend to a lack of concern and questions that had probably made him look cold in the face of everyone else's concern.

In the face of the shoe itself.

Because it did have a face, this shoe—a little orange clownfish face, cleverly painted on the worn sneaker to disguise the hole in the toe. Orange felt-tip pen, black markings made with something finer, maybe a laundry marker, and white edgings of correction fluid. Alice had always had a talent for drawing, and for improvisation...

'It was her sister I knew,' he'd said about Janey, in the A and E department, the night she'd been brought in. He hadn't said, *This patient's my sister-in-law*.

And it wasn't Frankie Jay's shoe, he told himself yet again.

It couldn't be.

The mysterious silent kid could not be Frankie Jay.

Yet Frankie Jay's aunt had been on the bus. She was lying in Crocodile Creek Hospital right now, asking about Luke—*asking about a little boy, too*?—but the shoe couldn't belong to her nephew—*my son*—because the consensus around the hospital, from people who

knew about such things, was that the shoe must belong
to a four-year-old or thereabouts, and Frankie Jay would
be turning six in just a few weeks.

Luke wouldn't even recognise him, he knew.

He hadn't seen him since he was three months old.

'He's coming in to see you now,' Dr Wetherby reported to Janey.

Charles, she remembered. He'd asked her to call him
that, and he knew she was a doctor herself. Charles
Wetherby. In a wheelchair. Somewhat of a local legend,
she gathered. He was the hospital's medical director.

Her brain still felt fuzzy and disoriented, slow to
process what was happening around her and the things
people said, struggling to make sense of everything.
But she kept trying, deeply anxious to return to full
health, to get out of here, although she didn't know
where she and Felixx would go.

Felixx, who was coming in to see her now.

'Georgie Turner's bringing him,' Charles continued.
'Our obstetrician. She's terrific.'

'He's been staying with her since the crash.' She still
had blanks in her memory, and forgot things she'd been
told.

'That's right.' Dr Wetherby was very patient. 'She
and Dr Carmichael risked their lives to find him and
Max, right in the teeth of the cyclone. We're all devoutly
thankful that the four of them survived.'

'How long have I been in here now?'

'Since Saturday night. And now it's Tuesday. You
missed all the drama.'

'Not all of it.'

Except that she couldn't remember. She and Felixx

had been on the bus that had slid off the road. There had been a landslide, triggered by the massive dump of rain that had heralded the cyclone, apparently. She remembered when they'd left Mundarri a few hours earlier, trying to get her waif-like, silent nephew to say goodbye to Raina and Maharia, but as usual he hadn't said a word, just waved, taken Janey's hand, stretched his small legs to climb the bus's high steps.

And that was all.

After this, everything remained blank, and when she'd regained consciousness, she'd had to ask, 'Where am I?' like an accident victim in a bad movie, before she'd remembered finding Luke Bresciano's contact details at Mundarri among Alice's things. The second thing she'd asked had been, 'Where's Felixx? My—my little boy.' Because, for the moment at least, he was hers.

'Is he OK?' she asked now, having been told at first that he was but not quite daring to believe it.

'Well, we have a couple of concerns…' Charles Wetherby said.

'Is he speaking?'

'No, he's not, and we were wondering if there's anything you can tell us about that. He doesn't seem to have a hearing problem.'

'He hasn't spoken to me either.'

'Since when, Janey?'

She frowned and tried to will the fuzz out of her brain. Since when? Since ever! But had she managed to explain…? No, that's right. They would have assumed the obvious relationship, and she'd been too fuzzy to correct them. 'He's not my son,' she said.

'But I thought—'

'He's my nephew. My sister's child. I don't know

him very well. She— They believe in alternative healing at Mundarri. I don't know if you've heard of—'

'Mundarri? Some kind of spiritual retreat, up in the rainforest?'

'That's right.'

'Well, I do think there's a place in our system for alternative medicine…'

'I do, too, sometimes.'

'But I've heard they have some odd ideas.'

'Odd ideas that killed my sister.' She sketched out the story as briefly as she could, sidetracked into an ambush of emotion before she could swallow it back, and even just that amount of effort tired her out. 'I'm sorry, I'm a doctor myself. Right, yes, I did tell you that.' Her head hurt. 'As you say, I think alternative healing has its place, but—'

'We're both doctors, you don't have to explain.'

'Will I be discharged today?' she asked, knowing the answer even before she heard it.

'Not before tomorrow, I shouldn't think,' Charles said gently. 'Should we postpone your nephew coming in?'

'Oh, no, please. I want to see him! Let me just close my eyes for a minute…'

And the next time she opened them, not long afterwards, there he was, being ushered into the room by an attractive and very energetic-looking woman with bright red dangly earrings. She had a pretty impressive bruise on the side of her face, which Janey put down to the cyclone.

'Felixx…' Janey struggled to sit up, struggled yet again not to cry. She didn't want to scare him any more than he'd been scared already by all that had happened, all the uncertainty, all that he'd lost. 'Oh, sweetheart… Oh, darling…'

She held out her arms, but Georgie Turner had to nudge him forward. 'Come and hug your Auntie Janey.' Charles Wetherby must have explained their relationship to her.

At last he came, and she felt his warm little body. Had a momentary flashback to the bus. That's right, he'd fallen asleep on her shoulder, so warm and trusting and relaxed. Now she wanted to hold him for ever, just for the reassurance that they were both alive, that she hadn't let him down, that they were together, so everything would be all right.

But he pulled back.

Didn't speak, of course.

Why didn't he speak?

He looked scared. She could see him taking in the equipment—the drip stand and bag of fluid and cannula taped to her hand, the monitor reporting on her oxygen and heart, and the imposing side rails and wheels and crank handle of the hospital bed.

Alice, she remembered. He was scared because his mother had died, and now his Auntie Janey was ill, too.

'I'm feeling so much better, Felixx,' she said quickly. 'Dr Wetherby says I can probably get out of here tomorrow. I'm sitting here going woo-hoo!'

On Felixx's face the sun came out from behind a cloud. It was the only way Janey could describe it to herself. His smile spread wide, his eyes went happy, his tense little shoulders dropped and relaxed. He looked as if there was something else he wanted to say or ask, but didn't know how. Or didn't dare.

'Were you scared I was really sick?'

He nodded, cautious about it.

Oh, hell, of course he had been scared!

'Nah,' she said, deliberately casual and dismissive. 'Takes more than a few bumps on the head to knock me around. We'll be able to check into a nice motel, and—' She stopped.

Georgie was shaking her head. 'No motels,' she mouthed.

The cyclone, Janey remembered. As she hadn't seen it or heard it or even seen the damage yet, she had to take it on trust and her foggy brain kept forgetting. None of the motels in town were currently open for business apparently.

She put on a bright voice. 'Well, we'll have to camp or something.'

'If you're not feeling well enough to travel yet, Janey, we can arrange something. There's a big house—it's the original hospital building—where several of the doctors live, and we can usually find extra room.' Georgie's bright earrings bobbed as she talked. She looked like the kind of woman who could arrange emergency accommodation on an uninhabited planet if she had to. 'We can lend you some clothes. Rowdy, here, was pretty happy to be reunited with his missing clownfish shoe, but his toes are getting squashed in those sneakers, so we've found him some new ones.'

'You haven't thrown the clownfish shoe away?'

'Ooh, no, weren't allowed to do that!' Her face telegraphed the story. Rowdy must have clung to the shoe. Alice had painted the fish on it to hide the hole in the toe, Janey knew, and of course he wanted all the reminders of his mum that he could find.

'Thanks,' she said, her voice husky with tears.

'To be honest, though,' Georgie said gently, 'getting back to the issue of where you're staying, we're encouraging people to evacuate if they can. Resources are pretty stretched. I think the Golden Palm will be up and running in a couple of days. It's not exactly five-star, but they only had minor damage and they're working on getting one block of rooms back into a fit state for guests. There's the Athina, too, but that'll be full. They've just had a big wedding. You're from Darwin?'

'I don't know where I'm from right now.' Janey closed her eyes. 'The moon?'

The thought of finding a place to stay, tracking down Luke, presenting him with his son and saying something like, *Do you want him? Alice said you didn't, but she's gone now, and I'm wondering if that might make you change your mind. After all, you are the only father he's got...*

Exhausting.

Too hard.

She'd asked someone about Luke, but maybe no one had passed the message on. Or, no, with services in the whole region so strapped, he'd be working around the clock, playing the hero.

He had a nice line in heroic behaviour. People loved the casual humour, the god-like reassurances and the warm fire in his amber-brown eyes, and immediately believed in him. She knew what he was like...or had known once... He wouldn't be able to resist the opportunity to show off in all this chaos. Which was good, because she didn't have the energy for their confrontation just yet.

'Honey, we might take you back to play with Max, OK?' she heard Georgie say. 'Auntie Janey needs to rest for a while now.'

He stood there looking at her for a moment,

frowning, giving off that same sense that he was about to speak, that the words were just crammed in his mouth bursting to come out, but as usual he stayed silent.

'Bye, sweetheart,' she managed, then the sleepy fog stole over her brain again, and hours passed.

The next time she woke up, her head had cleared, her stomach wanted food, her limbs were ready for a good stretch and altogether she felt about a hundred years better.

Until she became aware of the quiet masculine presence in the chair beside her bed—dark hair, strong shoulders, genuine, implacable fatigue written all over him—and realised it was Luke.

CHAPTER TWO

LUKE looked exhausted and stressed.

He had bloodshot eyes, hair yelling for a brush, even a streak of dried mud along his jaw. He looked older. There were some lines around his eyes and mouth. Janey hadn't seen him in, what, seven years? No, just under six, if you counted photographs.

Alice had sent one from London shortly after Felixx's birth—a casual shot of both parents and the tiny bundle of baby snuggled between them. Alice had looked tired, but Luke had glowed—the archetypical proud father. Just three months later, their marriage had shattered. Janey still didn't know the full story, and what she did know had come only from Alice.

So how did you even start in a situation like this?

With 'hello' apparently.

Luke said it first, his voice low and tired and husky. Despite the changes in his appearance, he was still the man she remembered, dark and ferociously good-looking, with those trust-me-I'm-a-hero amber-brown eyes and a confident mouth that had rarely bothered to bestow its charming smile on Janey. She'd seen it quirked in annoyance or outright anger far more often.

'Hello, Luke,' she answered him. 'It's good to see you.'

His smile was strained. Good to see each other? Maybe. And they both looked wrecked. He carried his fatigue well, but she had no illusions about the appearance she must present after two days of unconsciousness in a hospital bed—and she'd never been the pretty one of the two Stafford girls.

'It's been a while,' Luke said.

'Too long.'

His face changed. The strong jaw suddenly looked harder. No charm in evidence at all. 'Don't put that down to me, Janey. Just don't. I contacted you and your parents over and over, asking you to put me in touch with Alice, and you insisted you didn't know where she was.'

'We didn't, then. She didn't contact us for a couple of years.'

'But you do now?'

'It's complicated...'

'Explain, Janey. Pretend I'm completely in the dark, no idea what's been going on for the past five and a half years with my wife or my son. Just pretend, OK?' His voice dripped with harsh sarcasm on those last three words.

Oh, lord, their dealings were getting badly strained already, and she had some shattering news to impart!

I won't do this, she vowed. I won't make it into a battle or a litany of accusations, no matter how I feel about Luke, or how much truth there might have been in what Alice said! Felixx has endured enough, he doesn't need his two closest living relatives to be at war with each other.

It wouldn't have been Alice's approach, she knew. Alice had loved the high drama of family arguments and taking sides and emotional manipulation. You became drawn into it, inevitably, because—like Luke—she had so much charisma, so much life, so much self-belief. The world always seemed a more interesting and dramatic place when she was around.

Had loved.

Had had.

Had seemed.

Luke must have seen something in her face. 'I'm sorry. Shall we start again?' he said.

'Let's.'

'I'm sorry,' he repeated. 'I can't do the small talk. Not in a situation like this. There's only one thing I want to know right now. The child. The boy. He's around four years old, people are saying. They've been calling him Rowdy, but you've said his name is Felix. So he's your son. I had this stupid hope for a while that—' He broke off.

The look on his face was that of a man still under torture. It shocked her, because she'd never seen him like this before, wouldn't have said he had the capacity to feel life's darker emotions so deeply.

He was the sunshine type.

'Luke… Dear God, I thought you knew,' Janey blurted out. 'He is Frankie Jay. He is yours. Of course he is.'

She watched him try to stand then sit back down as if his legs had given out from under him. He looked totally bewildered. 'But—*Felix*?'

'Alice changed his name, and I've grown used to it. She changed hers, too, and both their last names. Alanya and Felixx Star. Felixx's has a double X, which is—'

Ridiculous.

She stopped. Why give this detail now? The double X. Her opinion of it. Her brain still wasn't working quite right. 'He's small for his age,' she went on. 'He does look like he could be four.'

Luke put his head in his hands for a long moment, hiding his expression. She wanted to reach out and comfort him with her touch, but didn't think she had the right or that he'd want her to. The nakedness of his re-actions kept surprising her, although she couldn't have put into words what she'd expected instead.

More of a performance?

'When they found your ID in A and E on Saturday night, I didn't know why you'd been on that bus,' he said eventually. 'If it was anything to do with me, if it was just one of those bizarre coincidences, or if Alice had put you up to it for some reason... Hell, I can't call her Alanya! Where is she? Was this her idea? Why bring him here now, after all this time, when she did so much—must have moved heaven and earth—to make sure I could never find either of them?'

'Never find them? She said you didn't want him! Or her. That you couldn't handle fatherhood and wanted your bachelor days back. That you were the one who left.'

'Which you instantly believed, of course.' Suddenly, they were both gabbling, fast and furious.

'Yes, because—' She fought the swimming feeling in her head.

'When was this?' he demanded. 'After my phone calls from London, or before?'

'You'd said when we were working together—and you said it more than once—that you never wanted kids. And you certainly used to enjoy your freedom. Some men find they can't deal with—'

'No!'

'Yes! When we were interns, those three months in the paediatric unit. We saw some heart-rending things.'

'All right, I remember. I was twenty-six years old. That's a young man's response, Janey, pretty unthinking in some areas, far too black and white. *I'll never have to see a child of mine go through this, because I'm damned sure now that I'm never having kids*. As for enjoying my freedom, that's just how you would phrase it, isn't it? The negative connotation. We all needed a bit of a release in those days. I changed. I loved Frankie Jay like— When was this? When did she say this? After my phone calls?'

'After, when she came back to Australia.'

'When you already knew how desperate I was to get in touch with her and see my son.'

'It's easy to say. Especially on the phone from half a world away. That you're desperate to get in touch. It's the expected reaction. Casts you in a heroic—'

He swore. 'You thought it was just a *performance*? Hell, I knew you never thought all that highly of me marrying your sister, but...' His lips had gone white. 'We worked together. I saved your backside a couple of times, and you even returned the favour. There was a degree of respect between us. Professional respect, at least. I thought. But that's what you think I'm capable of.'

'I wasn't accustomed to think my own sister was telling lies. I didn't know what to think or believe or feel. You know what she was like, Luke. She drew us all in.'

'Captivating,' he said bitterly. 'She weaves these beautiful, magical webs around her life. You want to be in her world because it looks so sparkling and wonderful. You believe every word she tells you. She casts spells. Wait a minute...' His face changed, and Janey knew he'd belatedly registered her use of that tell-tale word 'was'—the past tense.

'She died,' she told him simply. She swallowed. Luke didn't need to see her in tears. She'd shed enough of those when she'd first heard the news. 'A week ago. No, ten days. Oh, hell, nearly two weeks, I'm still in such a fog.'

She sketched in the medical facts for him, then continued, 'She was living at Mundarri, it's a retreat. A commune, some people would call it. And they didn't realise how ill she was until it was too late. Charles Wetherby knew of the place when I told him. Up in the rainforest. I don't know if—'

'Yes, spiritual healing, or something. I guess that fits. She'd begun to get heavily involved in that sort of thing in England before she disappeared.'

'Disappeared?'

'Just went off the grid, Janey. Do you think I didn't try every avenue I could think of to track her down when she took Frankie Jay?' His whole face blazed, and she could see the way his tightly held fists made his forearms knot with muscle. 'She did it deliberately, no matter what she might have told you. That would have been when she changed their names, not when she got to the rainforest place, Mundarri. And I wouldn't be surprised if she changed them more than once. Poor kid, probably doesn't know what he wants to be called. It wasn't me. I wanted our marriage. To try and save it, for his sake. I wanted to be a good father. She sabotaged everything.'

'Luke—'

'I don't use that word lightly, and the only reason I never spoke of it in those terms when I called you from London was that I thought if I sounded too harsh about her you wouldn't tell me where she was.'

'Why didn't you try again when you came back to Australia? I didn't even know you were back in the country until I found your contact details amongst Alice's things. She must have kept track of you.'

'While making damned sure I couldn't trace her. I gave up, that was why I didn't make contact with you or your parents when I got back. Maybe I shouldn't have given up. But it was killing me. I didn't get a senior fellowship in the US that I wanted, because of it. I was too distracted, trying to find my wife and child. The fellowship went to someone else, and deservedly so, because I hadn't been giving a hundred per cent and I couldn't fake it any more.'

Luke Bresciano? Unable to fake it?

Again, she let too much show on her face.

'Yes, you're right, OK? I did used to fake it sometimes, when we were interns.'

'Sometimes?'

'OK, a lot. Never the actual medicine, but the bedside manner, the confidence, sure! It was a survival strategy. We all had them. Apparently you weren't impressed with mine.'

'Finish the story, Luke.'

'I came home to Australia instead. I knew my son was at least safe, that Alice loved him. I decided that would have to be enough, the abstract knowing. I'm not the first parent to have lived through losing a child completely when a marriage breaks down—to have a son or daughter or a whole family just vanish out of your life, and your ex to go to incredibly extreme measures to deprive you of any contact. I joined a support group for a while, but some of the bitterness and desperation I saw in those other parents... No. For sheer survival I had to turn my back and start again.'

'Oh, Luke…' She slumped against the raised upper half of the hospital bed, her energy completely drained. Her hands were actually shaking, cold despite the tropical heat.

He reached out and covered her clammy fingers with his warm palm. Instinctively, she closed her eyes. The contact felt good, far better than she would have expected. It oriented something in her universe, and she didn't stop to think if that might be in any way dangerous.

Couldn't stop to think.

Didn't have any thought power left.

'This is too exhausting for you,' he said. 'I'm sorry. We shouldn't be talking about it now.'

'We had to. How could we have put it off? What would we have said instead?'

'Where is he? Will you let me see him?'

'*Let* you see him?' Her eyes flew open, she tried to sit up and saw stars.

His voice seemed to come from a distance. 'Your sister didn't let me, for over five years. Who has legal custody of him now?'

'I do, but it's temporary.'

'Your parents…?'

'Mum's not well. Dad's struggling, taking care of her. Alice's death has hit them hard. They couldn't manage a child now. They want me to have him, but—'

'You don't?'

'Oh, I do, with all my heart, but I thought you should have a say in it, Luke.' He was still holding her hand. Instinctively, she squeezed it. 'That you should have him, if you want him. I—I do trust that your heart's in the right place.'

He'd never been *bad*, after all. Just because she

hadn't liked him, just because he'd made her spit chips every time they met, and she had thought him so arrogant and immature... She wouldn't let personal feelings win out over the objective realities of right and wrong. He'd be a good father, if he wanted to be.

'All the stuff that happened with you and Alice...' she said, 'a bad marriage can bring out the worst in people.'

'We were never right for each other. We dazzled each other at first, but I wouldn't want those stars in my eyes again.'

'Luke, if you want Felixx...Frankie Jay...then he's yours. He has to be. It's the right thing. That's why I came to Crocodile Creek.'

Approaching the doctors' house where he'd lived for almost five months, Luke saw the place as if he'd never seen it before.

Because now, since Sunday night, his child had been here.

He'd left Janey to rest, knowing there were still a million things to say but that she was too exhausted for either of them to do any more talking at this point. In any case, the urgency to see his son was suddenly shattering.

It pulled him like a magnet, made him feel ill and dizzy. He couldn't live a minute longer if he didn't see his boy. A part of him still believed it would all turn out to be some nightmare mistake and the child wouldn't be his at all.

'He's sleeping on a camp stretcher on the floor in Emily's room,' Charles had told him a few minutes ago. 'Has been for the past two nights. I guess you really have been bedding down in the A and E department.'

'Yes. When I've slept at all.'

The whole town was in chaos. With the bus crash and cyclone barging in on their wedding reception three nights ago, Emily and Mike Poulos should have been miles away on their honeymoon by this time but instead they'd stayed to help. They'd had no choice in the matter, and it might be days longer before they could easily be spared and before regular commercial flights resumed.

The short snatches of time that Emily and her new husband did manage to spend together, they spent over at the Athina Hotel, in a room that was too rain-damaged for real hotel guests, with its sodden carpet ripped up, but quite acceptable to a couple of battle-weary doctors who happened to be newly married and madly in love.

Which meant that Emily's room had been available for Max and Frankie Jay.

I am not calling him by the name Alice used when she stole him away.

'Although I'm not sure what he'd be doing right now,' Charles had continued. 'Eating, probably. He's developed quite an appetite since we got hold of him.'

And when Luke tiptoed up the steps and into the big communal kitchen with his heart thudding right up in his throat, there he was. *His son.* Eating an enormous hamburger with everything, half of which—fried egg, beetroot slice, grated carrot, pineapple ring and cheese— was sliding out the sides and back onto the plate.

Frankie Jay had beetroot juice and burger bun crumbs smeared all over his face, and was tackling with serious attention the issue of how to get the fallen bits of hamburger filling back into his mouth. Via reinserting them into the bun? Or should he take a more direct route?

Luke simply stood and watched, totally overwhelmed, seeing bits of himself, bits of Alice and Janey and four grandparents and finally just the new, unique being that wasn't bits of anybody else but was just Frankie Jay. Dark hair, brown eyes, scratches and mosquito bites on his skin, freckles across his nose, wiry little limbs.

Georgie saw him in the doorway first, and she must already have been briefed by Charles as she raised her eyebrows in a question that said, Shall I let him know you're here?

Luke shook his head, wondering if the whole medical community—in fact, the whole town—knew by now that this was his long-lost son, and the owner of that forlorn little shoe. He'd kept to himself a fair bit since coming here. His shattered past would provide fascinating fodder for gossip. The thought stripped him raw, when he didn't know how any of it was going to work out.

Georgie nodded and stayed silent, and they both watched Frankie Jay eating. Only when his plate was cleaned of every last bun crumb and tomato sauce smear and lettuce shred did he look up. As if wondering about dessert. Hadn't Alice *fed* him up in the rainforest? No wonder they'd all thought he was only four years old, he was tiny! And, though wiry, he was thin.

'Had enough, Rowdy?' Georgie said cheerfully.

Rowdy?

That's right. He hadn't been speaking.

Why hadn't he been speaking?

So they hadn't known his name, the medical personnel who'd rescued him and checked him and brought him in, and the nickname they'd given him had apparently stuck. Luke found he quite liked it. It took care of the adversarial relationship in his own mind between Felixx and Frankie Jay, and provided a compromise that everyone could live with, at least for the time being.

Rowdy looked towards the doorway and saw him at last, then nodded slowly in answer to Georgie's question. He'd had enough to eat was the impression. Well, maybe. Because if the word supper happened to be mentioned a little later on, he wouldn't say no...

'Hi, Rowdy,' Luke said to him. He couldn't believe it was such a quiet moment when there should be trumpets sounding or a huge orchestra reaching a crescendo. In the back of his mind he realised it was no accident that so few people were around. Charles and Georgie had engineered this whole scene by sending everyone else away.

To protect my child? Or to protect me?

Both, he decided, and was grateful. It was good of them. Not something he had the right to expect when he'd kept so much to himself since he'd come to Crocodile Creek. Janey wouldn't believe that the charmer with the major ego from Royal Victoria Hospital could have morphed into such a workaholic loner.

'This is Luke, Rowdy,' Georgie said. 'He's...' She threw him a panicky look. What did Rowdy know?

'I'm a friend of your Auntie Janey,' Luke supplied.

Rowdy smiled. Apparently he liked his Auntie Janey.

'I've just been to see her.' An image flashed into his mind of the way she'd looked against the hospital white of her pillow. Vulnerable yet calm. Lips a little dry. Eyes huge and shadowed. Never anywhere near as beautiful as Alice, but a lot more grounded and with an intelligence she could never hide. 'She's still pretty tired, but she's doing a lot better.'

Rowdy pressed his lips together and nodded, and you'd have thought from his expression that Janey's recovery was all down to him, that possibly the entire universe would end if *this one kid* didn't breathe in the right way, or wipe his plate clean with the correct licked finger, or something. He had an air of crushing responsibility about him, and the pleasure of the hamburger was apparently already too far in the past to be of any help.

'Hey…' How did you reach out to a kid who didn't speak. *Why* didn't he speak? How did you create a bond, and trust, and a relationship?

Luke felt completely at sea. He'd been holding himself back for so long, he just wanted to unleash his emotions right now, on the spot. Crush his child in his arms. Say all these fervent, dramatic words.

I love you. I would die for you. I have missed you every single day. I taught you to laugh, do you know that? I used to blow raspberries on your tummy when you were three months old, and you used to gurgle and gurgle and laugh and laugh…

But he knew he couldn't.

What the hell should he do instead?

He turned back to Georgie, helpless and close to tears. 'I…uh…'

'Hey, shall we head outside for a bit before it gets dark?' she said cheerfully to Rowdy, who stood up at once. The weight on him seemed a little lighter again, but his silence was just as complete. She told Luke, 'We had a team clearing up around the pool area yesterday, so the kids would have somewhere to play. The whole town is doing it—creating tiny pieces of order in the chaos. The beach is still a mess, the sand half cut away and covered in debris, and the surf is brown.'

He grabbed her arm just as she was about to follow Rowdy outside. 'I don't know what to do, Georgie.'

She stopped in her tracks. 'You mean about the momentous reunion?'

'Yes.'

'Momentous isn't what he needs, I don't think.'

'I know it isn't, but what is there instead? It's momentous for me, and I'm having a hard time getting past that to what else I could—'

'Just…child care. Fun stuff. Minute by minute. Throw him a ball. Read him a story tonight. We have kids' books here. Take it slow. We can't swim yet, unfortunately, because the pool's still full of debris and muck and chairs.'

'I'll clean it out tomorrow,' Luke said. It was a resolution and a promise. He knew he hadn't made himself a full part of the Croc Creek medical community in the months he'd been there. This felt like something he could grab hold of, something concrete that he could do. For Rowdy. For his fellow doctors. For himself.

'Big job.' Georgie sounded sceptical. 'It's pretty gungy.'

'I want to.'

'I'd better dust off a bikini, then.' She grinned, then disappeared onto the veranda for a moment and brought out a big red ball. 'Here. Catch.'

With Georgie effortlessly starting the game, Rowdy was soon involved, throwing back and forth to Luke. He smiled, ran to retrieve dropped catches, followed instructions, once even laughed. But he said not a word, and that was hard. The game fizzled out after about ten minutes, and Georgie's pager went off.

'Rats! If this is that bloody Henderson baby, deciding to be born…'

Yep, apparently it was.

'I'll have to go, guys…'

'Where is everybody anyway?' Luke asked. It was getting dark now.

'At Christina and Joe's, having been told to eat their hamburgers somewhat faster than Rowdy did, and then we hustled them off. We thought—'

'I know what you thought. And thanks.' He dropped his voice. 'But it leaves us in a bit of a hole at this point, because… Would he stay with me, on our own?'

'You're a friend of Auntie Janey's. Does he trust…?'

'He doesn't know her that well either, but you saw his face when I said I was her friend. She counts for something, in his mind.'

'I'll get Alistair and Max to come back. You won't be on your own for long. He can get into his pyjamas and brush his teeth and there's a bookshelf in my room with those kids' books. I'm getting the impression he likes anything about trains.'

Rowdy had disappeared while they'd been talking.

They found him inside a few minutes later, in Emily's room, crouched by his camp stretcher and wolfing chocolate.

'Oh, sweetheart! You could have told us if you were still hungry!' Georgie said, stricken by the sight. He ate like a stray animal, as if he didn't know where his next meal was coming from. 'There's plenty more to eat in the kitchen.'

Rowdy looked scared and frozen, like a rabbit caught in the headlights of a car.

'Told us?' Luke said quietly.

'I treat him as if he talks, in the hope that soon he actually will,' she answered, even more quietly. 'We've taken a good look at him. There's nothing physiologically wrong. And he communicates. Doesn't usually initiate much, but nods or shakes his head, points.'

'He's so thin.'

'They have a vegan diet at Mundarri.'

Luke swore. 'It's hard enough for an adult to get a balanced intake that way, let alone a child. From the look of him, I'd say they didn't do enough.'

'Here, we're letting him eat what he wants so far. Don't want to turn him into a junk-food addict, but his protein and calcium and iron intake could certainly use a boost, and a bit of fat. For this week, chocolate is a health food.' She took a closer look. 'At least… Hmm, not sure about *this* chocolate.' She said to Rowdy, 'Where did you get it, sweetheart?'

Luke followed her deeper into the room, and they both bent down to Rowdy, who instinctively hid the chocolate in his hands.

'Show me?' Luke said gently.

He opened his son's fingers, to find the last couple of battered-looking, dirt-encrusted squares, then picked up the piece of torn wrapper he saw on the floor. It was soaking wet, as was the plastic bag it had apparently been stored in. He also found grit and clay and chocolate crumbs.

'Oh, shoot!' Georgie said. 'This is from Saturday night. The supplies Charles packed for us. We left it with Rowdy and Max, Alistair and me, when we had to wait out the worst of the storm. It's been through a cyclone, down a mineshaft and up in a chopper. Where have you been keeping this, Rowdy? Hidden here under the bed? You didn't have to do that! This is all dirty and gritty from the mineshaft, we should have thrown it away.

You can tell us when you're hungry, OK, lovey. I know, you don't like talking, but you can rub your tummy or point to the fridge. Eating isn't something we need to do in secret, my sweetheart! Never, never!'

She took the last few squares of chocolate out of a sticky but quiescent little hand, gave him a quick, reassuring squeeze and stood up.

'I really need to go,' she said to Luke. 'I'll phone Alistair on my way across and he'll be home with Max in a few minutes. Find a story to read, and don't give him a hard time about the chocolate.'

'You think I would?'

'Sorry. Bossiness gets to be a habit.'

'Thanks for it, Georgie. You've…helped tonight.'

So she left, and Rowdy didn't seem to mind, and Luke found a Thomas the Tank book, suggested pyjamas, teeth-brushing and toilet, then sat on the uncomfortable edge of the camp stretcher while Rowdy tucked himself under the thin summer sheet and they read about naughty trains.

And it was OK. It was good. They'd made a start.

Max arrived in the middle of it and heard a second story. Both boys yawned. Alistair appeared back in the doorway and said, 'Lights out, I think.'

No protests.

'Night-night, guys,' Luke said.

And that was it. His first evening with Frankie Jay, aka Felixx, aka who knew what else, aka Rowdy.

No dramas. Taking it one step at a time.

Pretty good, on the whole.

Until he got woken up at midnight by the commotion coming from Max and Rowdy's room.

CHAPTER THREE

'SHE'S asleep,' Janey heard, in her doorway.

The room was dark, and the patient in the next bed was just a humped shape who didn't stir. It must be very late. She tried to rouse herself enough to call out that she wasn't asleep, but the voices had already passed along the corridor. They must have met up with someone else at the far end. She caught snatches of words.

'Out of nowhere…'

'What Rowdy ate, but Max seems fine…'

'Don't want to set her back, but she's the closest thing to a parent…'

'Paediatric bed when we've…'

She struggled to sit up and make sense of what she'd heard. She couldn't, except to realise that it had something to do with her.

And Rowdy.

That name was going to stick.

It had stuck in her heart, because she so much wanted him to be a rowdy, noisy, boisterous kid, just to show that he knew how to. It was so frightening, his silence. She knew something had to be deeply wrong.

Something's wrong.

And not just because her nephew didn't speak.

I have to find out.

She pivoted her legs off the edge of the bed. Fortunately one of the side rails was down, because she didn't think she could have climbed over it. OK, now, drip stand. Handy things, they were. She held herself to it for support and pushed onto her feet, made some shuffling steps towards the electrical socket where it was plugged in, had to untangle the orange cord from around her buzzer and TV control and gather it into the little plastic loop on the stand, so it didn't trail on the floor.

She'd been out of bed twice that day. The first time she'd progressed all the way to the chair that sat four feet from her bed, then back again. That evening they'd taken out her catheter and she'd managed a bathroom visit.

But she'd had help.

This time she didn't.

'They are discharging me tomorrow, come hell or high water, so I'd better be able to do this!' she muttered. And as she took each tentative step, still clinging to the drip stand, the lightheadedness subsided and she felt steadier.

At the end of the corridor the knot of people still stood, talking. Luke saw her first, and she didn't take in who the others were. 'Janey!' He strode in her direction at once.

'What's wrong?'

'You shouldn't be out of bed.'

'Is it Rowdy? I heard—'

'He's been vomiting. I've just brought him in. But you shouldn't be standing here like this.'

'Where is he?'

'Downstairs, in A and E.'

'What are you thinking is wrong? To bring him in just because he's vomiting…'

'Let me grab you a wheelchair.'

'I don't need one. I want to get out of here tomorrow, so I'd better be able to walk down a level corridor without dramas! Take me down to A and E and tell me what's going on.' She dragged on his arm, aware of its warm, bulky strength, and he relented, leading her towards the lift.

'Joe Barrett's with him,' he said.

'I haven't met— But I've heard the name.'

'New Zealand doctor. Christina's husband. You wouldn't know her, either. It's not important right now. Rowdy's showing some other symptoms, that's our concern. Restlessness, headache, dizziness, chills, cramps.'

'Flu,' she guessed. 'A gastric bug?' What else might it be? She tried to think like a doctor, but couldn't do it right now when it was this little boy, almost her own. 'He's having such a horrible, horrible, time. Has anyone else—?'

'No, that's the thing. It's just him.'

They went down in the lift. She caught sight of a clock on the ground floor. One in the morning, no wonder she felt disoriented. *If I let it show, they won't let me out of here tomorrow. They'll keep treating me like a patient, and I need to be the healthy one, for Rowdy.*

'What are you thinking, Luke? You're not telling me.'

They reached the heavy swing doors that must lead into the A and E department and he stopped, faced her and stood close. 'We found him eating some chocolate this evening. Georgie had several bars with her when she and Alistair found Rowdy and Max down the mine-shaft, and she gave it to them for emergency rations. The boys ate half of it, but Rowdy hid the rest, and we didn't know. The wrapper was sodden and filthy, and the chocolate itself was covered in clay and grit.'

'I don't think he's ever eaten chocolate in his life. Alice was too strict about food. Way too strict.'

'Well, he's making up for it now. He was like a stray dog when we found him in his room, Janey.' His voice cracked suddenly, and he'd made a vivid, disturbing image in Janey's mind. 'Wolfing down this filthy stuff as fast as he could get it into his mouth, grit and wet wrapping and all.'

'Upset stomach…' She felt a little better. A bit of damp, dirty chocolate. He'd be fine. Miserable for half a day, but soon fine.

'No, that's not what we think,' Luke said. 'Those old mineshafts are a mess of half-dug holes and piles of tailings. They processed some of the gold on the spot. The soil's contaminated. We think it could be arsenic poisoning.'

Janey's knees buckled and Luke had to catch her before she fell. He felt the ridge of plastic from her IV line against the inside of his arm, the tied tapes at the back of her gown, and then the gap—those gowns never met properly behind—the warm gap and the smooth skin of her back. He rested his jaw against the top of her head. Her hair was silky and dark and fragrant, even after several days in hospital.

'We've taken a urine sample for testing,' he said. 'Meanwhile, we're going to treat it as confirmed. Gastric lavage, saline cathartic. If we get a positive result on the urine—they're pushing the testing on that through as fast as they can—we'll start dimercaprol for two days then penicillamine, as well as treatment for dehydration and pulmonary oedema and anything else we need to.'

'Haemodyalisis,' she said.

'Hopefully not, because we're not equipped for that here. He'd have to go south. I'm sure it won't be that severe. It won't be. It won't. This is acute, not chronic, and it developed fast and clear-cut because he's so small and we'll get it out of his system just as quickly.'

The words were a prayer, a threat and a promise all in one, and they both knew it. She held him more tightly, burrowed her forehead against his shoulder, and he felt her warm breath and the vibration of her muffled voice against his shirt. 'This is not fair. This is just not, not, not fair! He's been through so much already, Luke! I can't bear it. And I don't know if I'm...*enough*. You know? Enough for him. When he's lost his world.'

She began to cry, shuddering sobs that shook her body all the harder because she tried to swallow them back and make them stop. Luke knew why. She wanted to be strong, and to prove to everyone that she was strong so they'd let her take care of Rowdy, instead of being stuck away in a hospital room of her own.

She somehow thought it was still just the two of them—she and Rowdy. She didn't trust or realise how much of a commitment Luke had made in his own heart. She still thought he was giving a performance.

He couldn't spare the energy to be angry about it now.

'He has two of us,' he said instead, speaking as plainly as he could, hearing the frequent catches in his own voice. 'Never forget that. Never doubt it. I am here. I love him. I will do what it takes. Anything it takes. Every single day. I am his father. And I'm not going away.'

They were the words—some of them—that he'd wanted to say to Rowdy himself the previous afternoon, but hadn't been able to. And suddenly it was immensely healing and good and important to be saying them to Janey instead, because if they shared nothing else, the two of them, they shared a commitment to putting this child first.

She lifted her head from his shoulder and looked at him. No, *searched* him, his whole face, in quest of truth. He met her gaze full on, knowing she wouldn't be able to find even a trace of insincerity or hyped-up promises. He'd meant every word.

Finally, after what must have been almost a full minute, she gave a tiny nod, pushed back from his chest, then turned to the button on the wall that opened the swing doors. 'I want to see him.'

He was as white as a ghost, his breathing seemed shallow, and he'd just finished throwing up into a pale green plastic kidney dish. His nurse whisked it away, then came back to note the volume on his chart. His restless limbs twitched against the sheets, which were already untidy.

'Frankie Jay…' Janey whispered. 'Rowdy, love…'

The nurse—an older woman, Luke didn't know her that well—was getting ready to put in an IV. 'I'll do it,' he told her, then wondered if that was a mistake. This was his son. Nobody liked to treat a patient they were this close to.

But he did it anyway, concentrating fiercely on the little hand, finding a vein with his fingertip, sliding the needle in. The vein snaked away from the needle point and he had to try again. Rowdy must already be dehydrated, because his veins shouldn't be this flat. He'd barely winced at the pain, brave little lad, but Luke knew it must have hurt.

And would hurt again, with his second attempt.

This time, thank goodness, he found the vein and taped the cannula in place, attached the tubing, set the flow rate, told the nurse what drugs needed to go in, and wrote it all down.

Sitting in the chair beside Rowdy's bed and holding his free hand, Janey watched every move Luke made. 'How are you feeling, sweetheart?' she whispered. 'Please talk to us and tell us. No? You need to stay quiet? That's fine… That's fine…'

What else could she say?

Time passed, the way it did in hospitals. Uncomfortable and quiet and slow. She must have dozed for a while. Some movement beside Rowdy's bed awakened her, but Luke seemed to have gone. Instead, there was a man she didn't know, holding out his big hand for a shake and telling her, 'I'm Dr Barrett. But make it Joe, won't you? We have the result of Rowdy's urine test.'

'And…?'

'Confirmed.' He didn't use the word 'poison' and Janey was grateful. Rowdy looked as if he was sleeping, but you could never tell, and he was scared and lost enough already. 'Poison' was a frightening enough word for an adult to hear, let alone a child. 'We'll keep testing to watch for a drop in the level.'

'So you're going to start…?'

'Dimercaprol and penicillamine.' He was working as he spoke, noting down the new treatment, preparing the drugs.

'Where's Luke?'

'Getting you a wheelchair.'

'I don't need one. I'm staying here.'

'Wrong,' said Luke himself from the doorway, wheelchair in tow.

'I—'

'Unh-unh-unh!' He came forward and touched the tips of his fingers to her mouth in a warning. 'Do I have to tell you that you won't be discharged tomorrow—actually, it's today—if you're looking like a wreck in the morning? He's sleeping now. And he needs you to be fit when he's discharged. I am taking you back to your room, Janey, where you will sleep until you wake up on your own—no six o'clock hospital breakfast—and about midmorning, or maybe noon, a whole clutch of doctors will check you out and pronounce yes or no. What do you want it to be?'

'I want yes.'

'Thought so. Need help getting into this wheelchair?'

'No!'

Why had he asked? He ignored her answer, bent down and raised the wheelchair footrests, lifted her to her feet, pivoted her round and held her elbow while she lowered herself. She wanted to say good night to Rowdy, kiss him and tell him she'd see him as soon as she could, but Luke was right. He was sleeping, and it was best to leave him undisturbed.

As they wheeled their way toward the lift, she knew she was leaving half her heart behind in the paediatric section of A and E, where they were keeping him because so much of the hospital was in chaos. With some wards storm-damaged and out of action, and patients moved to wherever they would fit, the paediatric ward didn't have a spare bed.

Luke stayed with his son all night, watching every setback and every turn for the better. Rowdy was passing urine through the catheter the nurse had put in, which was good because lack of urine output could indicate that the arsenic poisoning was more severe. The fluid kept going in nicely, along with the dimercaprol, which would bond chemically to the arsenic and neutralise its effects.

The purging brought on by the emetics Rowdy had been given should get the undigested arsenic out of his system so that the level didn't increase. They'd test his urine again in a few hours.

Meanwhile, there wasn't a lot do except sit and watch, but somehow the weary passage of early morning hours seemed so precious and important. Making up for lost time. Healing all those terrible months and years of not knowing where his child was, of feeling Alice's disappearance with their baby like a punch in the face.

He still didn't fully understand what had gone wrong, how they could have gone from giddy, effervescent happiness—shallow-rooted happiness, he'd come to think—to so much fighting and distance in so short a time, less than three years between when they'd first met and when Alice had walked out.

Most couples did find that their relationship changed after the birth of a child. Was that where it had started? He remembered the day she'd come home from her new mothers' group when Frankie Jay had been six weeks old, full of some terrible secondhand story she'd heard about infant inoculations gone wrong. 'We're not having him immunised, Luke. I won't take that risk.'

'So you'll take the risk that he dies of diphtheria or whooping cough instead? Do you have any idea what the infant mortality rate used to be before those vaccinations were started?'

'That's right, Luke, hide behind the sterile façade of

Western medicine straight away, without even hearing the facts!'

'The facts? Have you actually looked at the facts?'

They'd had a huge fight.

But he knew that this had been the end rather than the beginning of the trouble.

He couldn't pinpoint the steps on the journey after all this time, but he'd learned that nothing could be quite as sour as dried-up chemistry, especially when you discovered that there was no respect or appreciation or shared understanding lying beneath it.

He would have kept trying, but maybe Alice had been the one to see things more clearly at that point. The marriage couldn't have been saved, and she'd known it sooner than he had.

His thoughts swung back to the present, and he realised with a wash of horror that Rowdy probably still hadn't had his immunisations. Look at his skin, all cut up and scratched. How could Alice have done it? How could she have taken him out there into the wilderness with no tetanus shots? He'd get one as soon as it was safe, and the other shots he needed, as soon as this first crisis was safely over.

First crisis?

Fourth. Fifth. Luke had lost count.

Alice's death, the bus crash, the cyclone...

His little miracle, that's who this precious child was.

My miracle boy.

Emotion overwhelmed him suddenly, and there in the dark, quiet hospital, he just sat there and let the tears come.

When Janey woke up, it was eleven in the morning, and she found Luke standing at the end of the bed.

The sound of him coming into the room had stirred her out of sleep.

'How is he?' Her voice croaked.

'He's turned the corner.'

'Oh, that's wonderful. That's so good.'

'The arsenic level in his urine is down already, no more vomiting, he's nicely hydrated now, good clear chest. I think he'll be out of here tomorrow.'

Don't cry, Janey.

'One thing I wanted to ask, though. Did you find any immunisation records among his and Alice's things?'

'No. And I don't think they'd exist. She didn't believe in it. I tried to argue the case, but—'

'You too, huh?'

'I probably didn't argue hard enough.'

Their eyes met, and for a moment Alice's ghost stood between them, relishing all these lovely swirls of high emotion in the atmosphere.

'I couldn't deal with her, Luke,' Janey confessed in a rush. 'She exhausted me. I can't live on that level. Everything so passionate, and black and white. She was one of those people who just can't do life's small moments. It's all got to be huge. Even the way the two of you fell in love.'

At first sight, when Alice had come to the hospital to meet Janey for coffee. Alice and Luke had been engaged within three weeks, and married a few months after that. They'd spent the first year of their married life in Australia, then they'd gone to London.

'You can't just have a nice chat to someone,' she went on, 'you have to open up your whole soul. You can't just follow a vegetarian diet, you have to treat chocolate and ice cream and even cheese as if they're poison.'

'You can't just get a nice, civilised divorce, you have to change your name, take your baby and disappear. I know.'

'You loved her energy and her passion.'

'Once. But her passion was the real poison in the end. Beneath it, there was nothing we shared. I'd never want a relationship like that again.'

'I don't want to dwell on the things that made her impossible.'

'No. We have to think about Rowdy. His future. His wellbeing.'

'Which will get a boost with a tetanus shot and his other vaccinations.'

'And a bit more chocolate and cheese. Clean chocolate this time.'

And whole milk, some good red meat and fresh fish, lots of the fruit and vegetables and whole grains he'd been brought up on and liked, and the odd exuberant overdose of ice cream. Strawberry and mango first off, Janey thought, piled high in a waffle cone. She wanted to spoil him rotten in all sorts of ways.

'Hey, there are some doctors coming to see you in a minute,' Luke said.

'Sounds good. Can't tell you how much I'm busting to get out of here. Although I...really don't have too much of an idea what's happening in my life beyond this afternoon.'

'Give it time, Janey,' he answered gently. 'We've got a lot to work out. We're not aiming to do it all by the end of the week.'

CHAPTER FOUR

THE last thing Janey expected, when her discharge formalities had been completed, was that she'd be spending most of the rest of the day beside the pool. Luke wouldn't allow her to hover over Rowdy at the hospital, and deep down, although she protested at first, she knew it was the right thing.

They'd paid him another visit on their way out. He was looking a little brighter, sitting up in his bed and working on a jigsaw puzzle. It was hard to know how he felt about anything when he wouldn't speak, but he'd seemed more cheerful, obviously relieved to be feeling better.

Luke had said, 'Listen, little guy, I need to take your Auntie Janey away for a rest, and I need to get some myself. Doctor's orders. We had a cyclone here. I reckon you'd know something about that, right?'

A small nod. No smile.

'Well, we've all been working pretty hard, or else we got clonked on the head like your auntie did, and she needs to sit in the sun for a bit and get herself better. Get healed.'

He nodded at that last word and got the little spark

of questioning and hope in his eyes that Janey had seen once or twice before and wondered about. He suddenly looked as if he was desperate to speak—*desperate* to. Ask a question or tell them something of crucial importance or just yell.

And yet no words came.

She waited, smiled at him, squeezed his little hand between hers.

Come on, sweetheart. Nothing terrible will happen if you say it. Just spit it out.

But no.

And now, half an hour later, here she was relaxing in a borrowed swimsuit by the pool.

Watching Luke clean it.

He'd already removed about ten buckets' worth of leaves and other debris with a big net on a pole. He'd added some chemicals, cleaned out the leaf basket, pulled a plastic poolside chair from the shallow end, near the steps. Several chairs had been thrown into the pool before the cyclone, apparently, so that they wouldn't get turned into missiles by the power of the wind.

'I take it you're not going to let me help?' she said.

'Nope.'

'Because I have to rest, right?' She resisted the temptation to pull on the swimsuit to make it cover her better. Having spent the last three years dressing for Darwin's perpetual summer, she knew that when you acted as if you thought your neckline was too low, it only looked worse. Style was eighty per cent confidence and a relaxed attitude. Alice had apparently understood this from birth, but it had taken Janey a fair bit of living to work it out.

She had a few items of clothing rescued from the bus

crash, but no swimsuit, just casual tropical shorts and tops which hadn't yet been washed, and even though it was hot it felt good to get some air and sunlight on her skin.

'And because there's a science to it, you see,' Luke said. 'You probably don't even know what floculent is.'

'Did have the vague idea it had something to do with liver function.'

'I'm speaking in the context of swimming pools.' He poured in about a gallon of the stuff as he spoke.

'Well, this swimming pool certainly has a lot of context. Green, scummy context, from this vantage point, not to mention the floating branches.' She watched him lift another one out.

'And at least five more pool chairs, I'm told,' he said.

'You'd need to be told. Even after everything you've taken out, I still can't see to the bottom.'

'But once the floculent has taken effect, I am reliably promised it'll be crystal clear. Although I think there are a few other steps involved first. Waiting overnight and vacuuming or something. I've got all the instructions written down.'

'So you don't actually know anything more about the care and feeding of swimming pools than I do.'

'Not a whole lot. But my learning curve is steep.'

Just a throw-away line, with the grin to match, and yet it was true, she realised. All through their internship he'd been a quick learner—part of what had irritated her about him. No one should be able to make medicine look that easy!

He'd flaunted it, too, had shown off his sharp mind. The times he'd referred to yesterday when he'd 'saved her backside', as he'd phrased it. She remembered those. He'd handled himself like a magician, conjuring the right diagnosis or the right procedure like producing a rabbit from a hat.

'There you go, Janey,' followed by his charm-laden grin.

Through slightly gritted teeth, 'Thanks, Luke.'

'No worries. You would have got there eventually. Buy me a beer some time.'

She sensed he didn't show off any more. The past few years had changed him. He'd matured in ways she hadn't expected. He'd needed a steep learning curve in deeper and far more personal areas of his life, and he'd responded accordingly. It had been rather a humbling learning curve for him, probably.

She could imagine that for a man like Luke, it must have been a terrible shock and a bitter frustration to discover that his intelligence and charm couldn't win him anything and everything he wanted—that life wasn't nearly as easy and sunny and favourable to Dr Luke Bresciano as he'd once thought.

Alice had been unforgivably cruel.

But she was my sister, and I loved her, and I'll never see her again.

It was hard, such a mess. If you'd been angry with someone you loved, the anger didn't always die when that person had gone. It simply had nowhere to fit, and just hung around. It got all mixed up with the grief, so you had that to grieve over, too—the fact that your anger wouldn't let you go. As time went by, her heart would have to settle, surely, but right now…

She had to blink back her tears.

Luke removed several more branches, found the arm of another submerged chair and began to heave. His white T-shirt fitted snugly over his muscular frame and emphasised the tanned arms that a man of Italian extraction would have acquired effortlessly within a week of coming to Crocodile Creek.

As always, by contrast, Janey had carefully slathered herself in sunscreen and moisturiser, under no illusions about what would happen to her skin at this latitude. It was the same in Darwin, if not worse. Partially shaded by the poolside umbrella Luke had unearthed from beneath the veranda, she positively gleamed with lotion from her collarbone to her toes, and yet she loved the heat.

Thinking about his olive-skinned heritage, and wanting to distract herself from those circular thoughts about her sister, she asked on an impulse, 'Your parents, Luke, how are they doing?'

He hauled the newly rescued chair onto the pale sandstone of the pool surround and stopped work for a moment while it dripped in the sun. 'Pretty well.' Behind his sunglasses, she couldn't see his eyes. 'I only see them a few times a year. But we're getting on a little better now.'

Janey remembered that there'd been a rift. Mr and Mrs Bresciano hadn't liked Alice. They'd let it show, and Alice had been angry and hurt. 'If we're not welcome under their roof, then we won't go. See how they feel about that! Luke fully supports me. He's furious.'

In hindsight, Alice had always seemed to prefer burning her boats to working on a relationship.

'So Rowdy has two sets of grandparents!' Janey exclaimed. She really didn't want to keep thinking about Alice when Rowdy was the one who needed her. 'That's wonderful!'

'I never told them,' Luke answered.

She didn't understand at first. 'Well, you've hardly had time.' It was still only Wednesday, less than twenty-four hours since he'd learned the truth about who Rowdy was.

'No, I mean they never knew we'd had a child. I wanted to tell them, all through the pregnancy and after the birth. Thought it might help.' Heal the rift, Janey understood. 'Alice wanted to wait. She hadn't forgiven them for the way they disapproved of our marriage. And then she left, just decamped while I was at work. She left a note.' He quoted bitterly, '"It's over. Don't try to find us. I can't deal with you in my life any more. You crush my soul."'

'Oh, hell, Luke!'

'And what was I going to do then? Tell my parents that they had a grandson but that they might never see him because I crushed his mother's soul and so I didn't have a clue where he was?'

'I'm sorry…'

His mouth curved down at one corner. 'For what? Arranging to have coffee at the hospital with your sister that day?'

'So you remember.'

'Our first meeting?' His and Alice's. 'Of course I do! I was twenty-six years old and thought I had the golden touch. It never occurred to me that love at first sight doesn't always lead to happy ever after. That the occasional five-minute conversation where you check out each other's belief systems and long-term goals might be a good idea. That maybe this star-crossed lovers thing was, in fact, just a virulent case of—' He stopped.

Desire, Janey understood. Stars in your eyes.

'Yeah.' He reached a thumb and finger beneath his reflective sunglasses and rubbed his eyes.

There was a silence.

'So you have a lot to tell your parents,' Janey said at last. It seemed inadequate. 'Listen, will you please let me help with the pool? Otherwise I'm going to keep asking these awful questions.'

'It's fine. We probably need to get it all on the table. I'm not letting you help.'

'I could wipe down the chairs after you get each one out. These two are unusable as they are, all slimy. There must be some rags. Seriously, I hate sitting still when someone else is working.'

He looked at her and cocked his head to one side. 'Yeah, I remember that about you.' From family get-togethers in the year before he and Alice had gone to England. They'd had some biting exchanges, Janey and Luke, washing dishes together. They'd actually known each other quite well.

'OK, then,' he said, 'but only if you take a break every ten minutes to sip long, cool drinks.'

'So who's bringing me the long, cool drinks?' she asked slyly.

He laughed, and she felt the most ridiculous spurt of pleasure because she sensed that his laugh didn't come easily any more. It felt like a real achievement to have coaxed it out.

So Janey wanted long, cool drinks.

Luke left her lolling by the pool in the reclining outdoor lounger he'd retrieved for her from beneath the veranda. Watching from the window of the big kitchen to make sure she wasn't illicitly removing debris from the pool, he didn't even get as far as the fridge for several minutes. Just kept looking.

They'd bugged the heck out of each other eight years ago, had really got under each other's skins. He'd thought she was prim and stuffy in her attitudes to medicine and study and life, and clueless about her own attributes. It had driven him mad that she could have been almost as beautiful and scintillating and fun as her sister, if she'd had the slightest inkling.

He'd wanted to drag her in front of a mirror and yell at her, 'Can't you *see*?' Or play back recordings of the things she said and tell her, 'Listen to yourself! How much do you think people like being lectured to about the politics of Third World malaria treatment when they're having a Friday night drink? You don't *need* to act as if your brain is the only thing you've got going for you, because it isn't!'

Why did she have to hold herself so stiffly? Why did she dress to hide that fabulous Stafford figure, instead of showing it off? Why didn't every man she met know about her incredible hundred-watt smile? Why did she use her sharp mind to bore people rigid with her knowledge, instead of making them think or laugh? She had a sense of humour, but she so rarely used it. She was so bloody serious and tedious about the world!

She *frowned* at men, instead of smiling at them, the way some women frowned at grubby little boys. Just a few weeks after they'd married, Alice had said to him, 'You have to help me find a man for Janey, Luke. She's a fabulous person, but men don't see it, and it's just wrong.'

And he'd seriously tried. Thought about which of his single male friends she might go for—which ones wouldn't be too much the football-mad type, which ones had interests she might share.

They'd gone on three or four appalling double dates,

him and Alice and Janey and whoever, where Janey had obviously known she was being set up, and every time she'd looked at him he'd seen her thinking, *You low-life*! This *is the kind of man you think I'd want*? Meanwhile, his friends hadn't looked past the bad first impression, and who could blame them?

He couldn't remember which of them had called it quits on the double dating first. Janey had, he thought. That's right, she'd asked Alice to tell him please not to embarrass both of them any further, and he'd been deeply relieved.

Angry, too.

She'd had no clue!

Now it all seemed so long ago, and there she was by the pool, stretching her long legs in the sun, wearing a scarlet swimsuit borrowed from Georgie Turner that would have had her pulling at the fabric and crossing her arms over her chest eight years ago, because Georgie's swimsuits were…um…minimal.

And underwired.

And if Janey hadn't realised eight years ago that she had the fabulous Stafford figure, she knew it now. Just subtly. Satisfied about it, not showing it off. She looked more like Alice. And yet *not* at the same time, because she didn't have Alice's dangerous glitter and fire.

Janey would always be quieter, he guessed. Her confidence would always come from within, from a hard-won understanding of her own strengths and successes and the way to let them show. The confidence would get stronger as she got older, he sensed, and it would translate into a subtle glow, like old gold.

Lord, she'd probably be a complete and utter knockout when she was ninety-five!

He'd better do something about those long, cool drinks…

Checking in the fridge, he found bubbly mineral water and tropical juice, and remembered seeing a bottle of Campari lurking somewhere. He found it high in a cupboard and added a splash, as well as generous quantities of ice.

It wasn't enough.

He wanted to see her smile, tease her a little.

OK, how about pineapple and melon pieces? And someone had bought a bag of those paper cocktail umbrellas for some pre-wedding event of Emily's and then had forgotten to use them. They were sitting under the sink. He skewered the pineapple and melon on the pointy ends of the umbrellas and put the drinks on a tray, along with a whole platter of fruit and a greenish glass jug of iced water already getting nicely beaded with humidity. The ice cubes tinkled against the sides of the jug when he picked it up.

Yeah, this was the effect he was after.

Ridiculously overdone.

Sheesh, it felt good to do something frivolous and pointless just for the fun of it, to make somebody laugh.

Even when Christina Barrett, née Farrelly, showed up and caught him at it. She raised her eyebrows. 'Party?'

'Private pool-cleaning party. Pregnant people don't have to join in. But I can make you an umbrella drink.'

'Thanks, but I'm fine.' She added casually, 'Joe's not around, is he?'

'Hospital, I think.'

'Couldn't see him there.'

'Who did you ask?'

'Well, I didn't…' She winced and rubbed her back. 'How about Georgie?'

'Picking up Max from school. Left an hour ago, so I suspect she got roped in to some cleaning up.'

'Oh, school's open again already?'

'The primary school is, just a couple of classrooms,' he answered, 'but not the high school. They had pretty extensive damage, and they still don't have power, I heard. Come on, I think you need an umbrella drink.'

'Yeah, I probably do.'

He threw together another tropical cocktail, admittedly with less care than he'd taken over Janey's, and followed Christina out to the pool. She looked pregnant with a capital P today. She and Joe had come over from New Zealand three weeks ago, thinking they'd organise the sale of Christina's house in Crocodile Creek and have all the finances and legal formalities go through by the time the baby was old enough to travel.

It had been a sensible plan.

They hadn't counted on a cyclone.

Joe had been working all hours at the hospital, and the house had sustained a fair bit of damage. Grace O'Riordan wanted to buy the place, but Christina had reneged on the previously agreed price because of the new damage, and Grace was still recovering from her dramatic immersion in the floodwaters, so the issue couldn't be resolved just yet. Christina and Joe might be in Crocodile Creek for a while.

Janey and Christina hadn't met yet. Luke made the introductions, kicking himself inside for minding that the extravagant drinks had lost their wow factor, with Christina as a distraction. He hadn't been rewarded with Janey's really full-on gorgeous smile at what he'd done, and he was disappointed.

What's this about? I'd go that far for a smile?

'So you're in general practice, yourself?' Christina said to Janey. She sat on the end of the pool lounger.

'That's right,' Janey answered. 'Darwin. Pretty challenging sometimes. The way it would be here, I expect.'

'Um, and are your obstetric skills up to scratch?'

Janey looked a bit blank.

Christina added quickly, 'I mean, not to get too personal on very slight acquaintance or anything, but I was really hoping Georgie would be here and she's not, and I'm probably making a fuss about nothing, but would you mind having a feel of this baby and telling me what you think? Second opinion, because I don't trust my own skills right now.'

Janey got serious and put down her drink. 'You're not feeling movement?'

'It's not that. There's lovely movement. I just think it's the wrong way around.'

'It's got time to turn,' Luke pointed out. She wasn't due for another three weeks.

'Um, maybe…'

'Christina?'

'I've been having regular contractions for the past three hours.' In a suitably dramatic punctuation to her statement, her waters broke at that moment and gushed onto the ground.

And the baby was breech.

Janey never even had time to give her second opinion because Christina bent over and shoved a hand between her legs and cried out, 'There's a foot! Ouch, oh, *crumbs*! I can feel a foot pushing straight down! I'm sure it's a foot. Oh, this isn't supposed to happen! I thought I had hours to go! It's a first baby! First babies don't come fast! And I don't want it feet first! I'm going to have my footling breech baby on the pool lounger and I can't find Joe.'

'You're not having your baby on the pool lounger,' Janey said, squeezing Christina's shoulders. 'Absolutely not! Luke's bringing a car, I'm putting on this sarong Georgie lent me, we're getting you across to the hospital right now, and Joe will be there to see his baby born.' She gave Luke a prompting glance, as if to say, *So where's that car? Why are you still here?* And he departed, impressed.

Although not surprised. All of that borderline-pedantic intellect and frowning at men eight years ago had somehow transformed over the years into just the right brisk, tender, confidence-inspiring bedside manner, and Christina already sounded calmer. 'Right, right,' she said, breathless. 'And Luke can get the car within yards, can't he, as half the pool fence blew away...? And I probably have hours to go.'

'Now, about this alleged foot,' was the last thing Luke heard.

Joe met them in A and E, looking nervous and strained. 'Is it really a footling breech?'

'I did a quick check in the car,' Janey said.

It was a hospital vehicle, and Luke had thrown her a box of surgical gloves and a stethoscope from the bag of equipment in the front seat. They'd both told Christina the exam could wait until she was settled in the maternity unit, but she'd remained fairly panicky despite Janey's best attempts to sound soothing, and she'd wanted that examination *now*!

'She's fully effaced,' Janey continued, 'four centimetres dilated, nice strong foetal heartbeat, but there's a foot right there ready to pop out as soon as it can fit, which will be any minute. I don't think there's much chance we could get the baby turned at this point.'

'And it really hurts!' Christina gasped, in the building grip of a contraction. She couldn't stay in the wheelchair they'd found for her. She dragged herself out of it and leaned on its arm, waiting out the pain with deep, steady breaths. When it had faded, she asked, 'Where's Georgie?'

'Still at the school,' Luke reported. 'I just got her on her mobile. They're having an impromptu working bee, so they can get a third classroom open tomorrow. Georgie chipped in to help, and I think she's got Alistair practically rebuilding the playground.'

'Typical!' Joe groaned.

His big hands worked nervously together. He looked about eighty per cent imminent new father and twenty per cent seasoned medical professional, and the twenty per cent was busy remembering all the horror birth stories he'd ever heard, and adding a few bells and whistles just for fun.

You couldn't help it in a situation like this when you were a doctor. Janey did the same thing when anyone she cared about was ill.

'She's on her way, but she's pretty filthy,' Luke said, about Georgie, 'so she's stopping in at the house for a thirty-second shower. Christina, she wants you prepped for a Caesar, she doesn't want to take any chances on this. She'd deliver vaginally for a frank breech, she says, if you were keen on the idea and everything looked good, but not for this.'

Christina nodded, clearly relieved. 'A friend told me about the footling breech she had to deliver vaginally once. If I'd known I'd be in this situation, I would have blocked my ears and refused to listen. No, I want the Caesar! I'm not risking our baby's health or my pelvic floor!'

Joe squeezed her hands, then looked at Luke. 'You'll do the anaesthesia?'

'Sounds like a plan,' Luke answered. Janey looked a question at him—anaesthesia?—and he explained, 'I did some training in it when I got back from London, when I decided to work in rural medicine.'

'There's such a shortage of those specialties outside of the capital cities,' she agreed, inwardly impressed. His extra training showed a commitment to spending a serious amount of time away from the career-building centres of city medicine—not what she would have expected of the golden boy he'd been eight years ago.

'General or epidural, Luke?' Christina asked.

'Your call. We've got time to think about it.'

'Epidural. I want to be there, awake and alert, and I want Joe.' She gripped his arm and they exchanged an emotional look. He helped her back into the wheelchair and turned it in the direction of the operating theatres.

Luke nodded, then turned to Janey. 'Looks like I'm going to be busy for a while. Why don't you go back to your umbrella drink?' He glanced down at the borrowed red swimsuit and blue-and-white patterned sarong—glanced *appreciatively*?—and for the first time she felt self-conscious and distinctly underdressed. 'And drink mine for me, too, while you're at it.'

'I'm fine, don't worry about me, but isn't there anything I can do?'

'Janey, be sensible,' he said gently, and brushed the back of his hand across her shoulder and up to her cheek.

The contact felt so tender. He kept surprising her this way.

No, she kept surprising herself. Where was all that bristling irritation and cynicism she'd always felt about him? She missed it, for some reason. Had she *enjoyed* disliking him, then?

Hmm, she soon decided that she had. There was something safe and liberating in letting her negative feelings show, not trying to pretend. They'd both been pretty blunt with each other in the past. Now she wasn't quite sure where they stood, or how to deal with him.

'You're half a day out of hospital yourself,' he said. 'Someone can run you across to the house. You probably shouldn't try walking that far in this heat.'

But she didn't want to go back to the pool at the doctors' house, she wanted to see Rowdy. 'I'm going to sit with him,' she told Luke. 'Just sit, and see if...' If he might speak. She didn't say it out loud, but they both knew. 'Drop in and get me when you're finished.'

'Only if you promise you'll come quietly.'

She smiled and held up her hand. 'Promise.' Then she watched him effortlessly slip into the role of doctor as he strode rapidly away from her along the corridor, radiating confidence with every step. He used to do that eight years ago, she recalled. She'd found it absolutely infuriating back then—acting so macho, like he was God.

What had changed? Why didn't it get under her skin any more?

She didn't know.

'Looks great on you, Janey,' said a female voice beside her.

'You startled me!' Janey clapped a hand to her chest. It was Georgie, fresh from the shower with the ends of her short dark hair still damp and her surgical gear rather baggy on her petite frame. She stepped back and tilted her head, examining her own swimsuit and sarong on someone else. 'Seriously... Although it looks a bit tight in places.'

'You mean I'm practically falling out of it?'

'Nah, it's fine. Is there anything else I can lend you?'

'I've borrowed a couple of things from Emily. I'm doing very well.'

'Well, let me know, because I love seeing how my clothes look on other people! Must go. I hear Christina's baby hasn't read the right childbirth books.'

'No, definitely taking an individual approach to the process.'

Janey found Rowdy out of bed and playing with blocks on a bright square of carpet in the paediatric playroom. There was a little girl with him, about three years old, with a broken arm, a bandaged head and several dressings dotted around her body. They both had IV lines in their arms, tangled lengths of tubing getting in the way of their play, and drip stands like sentinels behind them.

They played in silence, occasionally nudging each other for a block or laughing when a tower fell down. The stands and tubing and silence both children treated as completely normal, but Rowdy looked scared about the laughing.

So peculiar, kids, the way they took things in their stride. They lived so much in the present, it had to be a protection for them against troubles that would overwhelm an adult. It was so hard to read what was troubling them underneath. *Why* was Rowdy scared to laugh?

Janey gave him a quick kiss and a hello and sat down

in a nearby chair. She didn't want to spoil this, because it had to be good for him. He looked so much better. If she were his doctor she would OK his discharge tomorrow.

But suddenly that idea was daunting.

Tomorrow meant the future, and a whole lot of questions she and Luke hadn't even tried to answer yet.

Tonight, they had to talk, she knew.

'Wriggle your toes, Christina,' Luke instructed.

'Can't.'

'Good. And can you feel this?'

'Nothing.'

'This?'

'No, lovely and numb, no sense of the contractions at all.'

There was quite a crowd in the operating theatre. Joe held Christina's hand and stroked the hair back from her face, muttering words of encouragement every now and then. Marcia and theatre nurse Jill did their bit with instruments and drapes. Georgie stood there with her hands deft and serious but her mouth acting as if they were all at a cocktail party. Luke kept an eye on various monitors and on Christina herself.

'So we're good to go?' Georgie said. 'Isn't this lovely? Crocodile Creek medics having a party. Want me to tell you what I'm doing, Christina?'

'You mean each layer of incision? *Now I'm slicing into your uterine wall.* Oddly, no!'

'You are such a wimp!' Georgie was, in fact, slicing into Christina's uterine wall at that very moment, but Luke didn't think the jittery patient had even realised she'd started the procedure.

'I know I'm a wimp,' Christina said. 'It's embarrassing. I should have a healthy clinical curiosity and switch to obstetrics the moment I'm back on my feet because the sight of my own innards has been so inspirational. I don't think so!'

'See, there's a reason why we drape you all across the middle so you can't see. Joe, how's that hand she's holding? Numb yet?'

'Just get the baby out, woman!' he said.

'We're getting the baby out. We're almost there.'

'You mean, you've been…?' Christina couldn't believe it.

'As we speak.'

'I can't feel it!'

'I think that's what we want, dearie, in this situation. Or that's what the instruction manual says…unless I'm on the wrong page.'

'Georgie, stop!'

'Ooh, yes, this is fun, I've found some knees. Might feel like you've got a bag full of fighting puppies on your stomach for a moment or two… Here we go!'

As usual, it happened very fast in the end. Georgie already had the baby in her hands, a dusky pink, slippery little bundle with a crumpled face and a fine fuzz of silky black hair, getting ready to howl at the top of its lungs after a fast and deft bit of suctioning from its nose and mouth by Marcia.

'Oh! Oh!' Christina said. She'd felt the pull.

'It's a girl, Christina, Joe, and she's beautiful,' Georgie said. 'Oh, listen to her!'

Yep, nothing wrong with those lungs.

Luke grinned, and then felt his throat tighten. He'd been present at Rowdy's birth, which Alice had chosen to have at home in their London flat. The home birth had made him nervous. He wasn't a big fan of the concept. He liked the philosophy behind it—of course birth should be the most positive experience possible, for both mother and child, and the father, too—but he didn't like the absence of a medical safety net if something went wrong. He preferred hospital-based birthing centres, where ideally you got the best of both worlds. But he'd swallowed his doubts, and in the event everything had gone fine.

It had been very different to this. Low lighting and music and scented oils, instead of the glare of the operating theatre, the rattle of the metal instruments and the chemical smells. And yet...did it really matter, underneath?

Georgie had clamped and cut the cord and laid the baby on Christina's chest. 'Oh!' Christina said again. 'Oh!'

She smiled and cried, her face rapt. She could have been in a primitive cave or an incense-scented room or almost anywhere, and her joy would have been just the same as this. Joe was grinning, his eyes shining with tears, too. The healthy-sized girl had stopped crying and looked quietly alert, with those muddy dark newborn eyes staring at the contrasts of light and dark and her little hands splayed out like pink starfish.

'Oh, isn't she fabulous? Oh, she's so beautiful!'

Luke checked his monitors and equipment, and thought that, really, in essence, this was no different to what he and Alice had had with their baby boy. The sense of love and wonder and enormous change. The instant perfection in those tiny toes, that silky head, those movements. Christina and Joe were captivated, bowled over, oblivious to everything else, and this healthy baby was already very deeply loved, and that was all that really counted.

This was Day One, just the beginning, and this little family was off to a good start.

'You might feel another bit of a pull,' Georgie warned. She delivered the afterbirth, checked that everything was intact, and Jill took the placenta away to be weighed. Shortly, they'd weigh the baby and check her for any problems. Luke doubted there'd be anything wrong. Her left foot was a little crooked because of her odd position in the uterus, but that shouldn't last, and could be corrected if it did.

'Congratulations, Christina,' he said. 'And Joe. Does she have a name?'

'Isabella Jane,' they chorused together.

'Just because we both like it,' Christina said. She dropped her voice and spoke to her little daughter. 'Don't we, sweetheart? Hope you do, too. Oh, I love you, I'm sorry I complained about your foot. It's a precious foot.'

'We'd better take her for a while,' Marcia said, after another few moments. 'She has a busy schedule this afternoon, don't you, sweetheart? She has to be weighed and measured and bathed.'

'And her mummy needs a bit of needlework,' Georgie said. 'Her seams have split.'

Christina laughed. 'Georgie, you are awful!'

'Careful about insulting your specialist while she has you flat on a table. I might use staples instead of soluble sutures, and then you'll be sorry.'

Luke shook his head and chuckled to himself. Then he thought about Janey and Rowdy, and realised that this was Day One for the three of them, too. His breath caught in his throat suddenly. There was so much to work out.

* * *

'Mr Connolly says you saw him on Tuesday at the emergency clinic in Bellambour and there was nothing wrong with him,' said Nurse Sarah Crisp in a tone that said, *This is your fault, but I'm the one copping an unreasonable patient.*

Her reaction made Luke officially sorry that he'd detoured through A and E on the way up to coax Janey away from Rowdy in the paediatric unit. He didn't unburden himself to Sarah regarding his failure to check Mr Connolly out properly on Tuesday. He'd tried to contact the Connolly family by phone three times now, but with the cyclone damage they didn't have coverage and he hadn't been able to reach them.

Still, it was his fault that the man was here now, apparently running a significant fever, with aches and chills.

He knew it was his fault, but Sarah didn't need a huge confession on the issue, not when Charles had told him categorically that he wasn't supposed to be working today.

So he attempted an approach that he rarely resorted to these days—a killer combination of arrogance and charm. Flashed the smile first then spoke, confident and breezy. 'Sarah, thanks for that. You're right. He's going to be a difficult patient. You know the type. Let me take a look at him, and I'm sure we can work out what's going on.'

But he couldn't do it any more.

It sounded tinny and wrong to his own ears, and Sarah didn't look impressed. He resisted the temptation to try harder and just let the subject go. He listened to Mr Connolly's chest and ordered an X-ray, told the man's daughter-in-law that he suspected pneumonia and then found Charles bearing down upon him. 'Luke—'

'Let me have this patient, Charles. It's something I should have picked up on Tuesday, and I didn't.'

'Come and talk in my office for a bit.'

'So you can tell me I've been working too hard? We hardly need your office for that!'

'So we can get a timetable sorted out, and your priorities. I know you're not going to leave the hospital in the lurch when we're so strapped, but you do need to take some time off.'

'I—'

'For Janey and Rowdy's sake, if not for your own. Do you know yet what's going to happen with the boy? We tend to take the future of our waifs and strays pretty seriously around here. What happens after he's discharged, as far as you're concerned?'

Someone walked past, ears clearly pricked to hear the latest news, and Luke dropped his voice. 'Your office was a good idea.'

'Mmm, yes, *I* thought it was,' Charles answered mildly, with a twinkle in his eye.

So I can still be a cocky young idiot, in some people's view, Luke realised, and had a sudden flash of understanding about why Janey had found him so unbearable eight years ago. Two minutes later he found himself spilling half his soul across Charles Wetherby's very nice antique desk.

And Charles listened. He was a good man and he had a lot on his plate right now. The hospital's administrator, Brian Simmons, whom no one much liked, had been away down south since before the cyclone had hit, and much of his workload was falling on Charles. Luke really had no right to expect such an attentive and empathetic audience but…yeah…he listened, and towards the end of it Luke found himself saying, 'I don't know if I'm the best person to have him. I'm his father. I love him.'

Charles nodded. 'I can see that. Isn't that all that matters?'

'But he doesn't have a clue who I am, and I have no idea if I should tell him, because I have no idea what Alice might have said to him about me. She was inclined to—I mean, it's the kind of thing I could see her doing. Telling him I was dead, or that I was a bad man, that I hated him and didn't want him. She told Janey I didn't want him. He seems to trust Janey. He knows who she is, at least, that she's his auntie, and he's happy about that. And she's such a great person. Grounded.'

'Yes, I've had that impression.'

'And I want what's best for my son. And maybe that's—' suddenly he was close to tears '—*not me*, Charles, if Alice has said all sorts of appalling things. After everything he's been through, maybe the best thing for my child is to let him go to Darwin with his Auntie Janey, and I can come and visit occasionally as a family friend, and Rowdy doesn't find out until he's an adult who I really am. If that's best…'

'But it's not what you want for yourself.'

'No. But does what I want for myself count, though? At all? I've seen parents shamelessly use their kids for their own ends and it's horrible. I won't do that!'

'You'd be a good father.'

'How can you possibly know that? I don't know it yet myself.'

'Because only a good father would say what you're saying. Is Janey settled in Darwin for good?'

'I have no idea.'

'Because if she's not, then you can reach a compromise, or take things slowly. Live closer to each other, for a start. One or both of you can move. It doesn't all have to be so black and white, Luke.'

'Black and white, that was very much Alice's style. I guess it's become a habit…'

'You're not Alice. And Janey's not Alice, as I understand it.'

'No, she's not.' He couldn't hide the heartfelt thankfulness behind the words, and he caught a curious glance from Charles.

'Here's what I prescribe,' the older man said. 'Go out to dinner tonight, the two of you, and talk. Find out what you're both thinking.'

'Dinner…' Luke said.

'The Green Dragon is open, in town. I recommend their Peking-style vegetarian dumplings.'

'Right.'

'Tomorrow, if I could possibly have you here at the hospital for a longish shift, I'd appreciate it, because I imagine Joe's going to declare himself on paternity leave for at least the next twenty-four hours.'

'Done.'

'We'll send Rowdy home to the doctors' house in the morning for some time with Janey, and then on Friday the two of you should take him somewhere. Charm Island is still in business, I'm told, and the resort shuttle boat service is running. Take a picnic, spoil him a bit, talk to each other when you can, you and Janey, and see where you get to after that.'

'What if—?'

'See where you get to,' Charles repeated. 'There might not be any what-ifs by then.'

Luke nodded, privately doubting. He had that old

feeling, the one he'd had in London after Alice and the baby had disappeared—that if he didn't do something heroic and physical and flashy and one hundred per cent proactive right this second, he'd actually explode, start yelling uncontrollably in the street and pulling out his hair, go stark raving mad.

'Saturday is Gina and Cal's wedding,' Charles went on. 'They insist they're not postponing it just for a little detail like cyclone damage.'

'Aren't they having their ceremony on the beach?' The lump in his throat had begun to get looser, thank goodness. It felt a little easier to focus on someone else's problems.

'Cal's organising a clean-up crew,' Charles said. 'Walter Grubb is handling the catering, which frightens me slightly, but he says the missus is telling him what to do and it's going to be a pit barbecue. It's not your problem. All you have to do is show up.'

'I have to do that?' He hadn't intended to go.

'With Janey,' Charles said gently. 'And Rowdy. Think he might be quite interested in a pit barbecue…'

'You might be right.'

They smiled at each other, and the weight on Luke's shoulders lessened a little further.

'How's he been?' Luke moved a spare chair closer to Rowdy's bed and sat next to Janey. She was watching his son sleep.

'He's been great!' She frowned and added in an undertone, 'For a kid who doesn't speak. He played toys with a little girl on the play carpet for, gosh, over an hour. He looked good, Luke, and he tired himself out in a healthy way, and now he's taking a nap. I'm just—'

'Watching him,' Luke finished. 'Yeah.'

They both did so, for about forty minutes, saying very little. It nourished something in Luke's soul, just to see that breathing going in and out, and that little face relaxed in sleep. Nourished him to have Janey there with him, too. When a child looked this peaceful, you couldn't believe there was anything really wrong with his spirit. If only Rowdy would speak…

'Charles has a plan for us,' Luke told Janey.

'Yes?'

'I'm taking you to dinner at the Green Dragon tonight.'

'Oh, you are?'

'We need to talk, don't you think? Easier if it's somewhere quiet, with no interruptions and nothing else to do.'

'That makes sense,' she murmured, and didn't argue, and as had happened when he had been talking to Charles, he felt a sense of the weight lifting from his tightly held shoulders.

Janey was sensible.

Good grief, he'd begun to value the fact that she was sensible!

CHAPTER FIVE

GEORGIE insisted on lending Janey a dress for that evening, but then Gina Lopez stepped in and said enthusiastically, 'Or why don't you borrow something of mine?'

She and Georgie fought with some degree of animation over whose clothes would fit Janey best, and who had the most appropriate outfit on hand for a scintillating evening at the town's venerable Chinese establishment. You would have thought that lending a temporarily homeless doctor some clothing was the must-do activity of the year. After a couple of minutes Janey began to foresee an escalation into mutual accusations of bad fashion sense and permanently wounded feelings.

'Let me stick to Georgie's wardrobe,' she said, 'because that's what we'd already agreed. I appreciate it, though, Gina, I really do.'

And she should possibly have considered the American doctor's offer more seriously, because Georgie's dressy outfits resembled her swimsuits in the skimpiness department. 'Who knew your legs were that much longer than mine?' Georgie muttered, surveying Janey's appearance in a sheath-style dress with a splashy abstract flower pattern of dark blue on white.

'It's fine. My legs'll be under the table.'

'Not in the car, they won't. They'll be right there in full view, all four hundred inches of them. I hope Luke can keep his eyes on the road.'

'It won't be a problem,' Janey said firmly.

And it wasn't. Luke's eyes stayed glued to the road as if he'd never driven before, and he seemed a little relieved when he announced, 'Here we are!'

He climbed out, looking strong and well groomed in his pale grey trousers and a white polo shirt which made his dark good looks even darker. It occurred to Janey that she'd be the envy of any woman who saw her, with a man like this beside her, and it gave her an odd feeling. Satisfaction mixed with a desire to run for her life.

Which made no sense at all.

'Mmm, smells good,' she said to distract herself as he opened the restaurant door.

She'd been out for Chinese food with him before, she recalled, on one of those awful double dates Alice used to push her into with Luke's male friends. She knew he liked spicy food, and trying new dishes. She also knew what he looked like when he was glowering at her because she didn't share his taste.

In men, not in Chinese food.

'I'm glad it's just the two of us,' she blurted out as they were shown to their table, then realised he wouldn't understand her thought track—he'd misinterpret completely—so made it worse by explaining, 'Those awful men you introduced me to on all those double dates, with Alice madly trying to demonstrate my intellect or what's-his-name's muscles.'

'They weren't awful.'

'Yes, they were! They were horrible occasions, every one of them!'

'I mean the men. You're right, the dates were bloody terrible, but Jack and Sean and Stephen are all really nice guys.'

'Well…'

'They're still friends of mine, Janey, so be careful.'

A chilly blast from the overactive restaurant air-conditioning hit her on her way past, matching the sudden chill of hostility in the air between herself and Luke. She bit her lip and swallowed her instinct to keep arguing. They couldn't afford to be at odds any more.

It felt familiar, though, arguing with him. Safe and satisfying, in a strange kind of way. She had a real struggle, letting it go.

'Do you see them often?' she asked politely instead. They'd been seated at a tiny table for two beside the ornately papered wall, facing each other.

'Not often enough, as they're down south.' He added quickly, 'Look, I appreciate that they probably didn't come across at their best on those evenings but, trust me, you weren't exactly the bachelorette of the year, yourself. You drove me nuts, Janey. I was so angry with you.'

'Oh, I'm telling you, that was so-o-o mutual! The way you—'

'Looking so prim when they told bad jokes. They were nervous, just trying to ease the atmosphere with some humour!'

'Showed off with them, all blokey and hearty and big-headed and full of yourselves. You were so immature!'

'And you acted like you were a middle-aged woman!'

'I was nervous, too, for heaven's sake! Alice used to give me these bright little pep talks about believing in myself, which made me feel as if there was nothing good to believe in. And you were so condescending, it was so obvious—to them, too, no wonder they wanted to run a mile!—that you felt sorry for me.'

'I *never* felt sorry for you! Just angry with you!'

'Why?'

'Because you were so much better and funnier and more interesting than you ever let anyone see, especially my friends.' He slammed the palms of his hands on the table for emphasis. His fingers were so long and brown. 'I sometimes used to think I'd only imagined that there was more to you than met the eye. You were bloody boring!'

'And you were an arrogant show-off, who thought you could wrap everyone you met, male or female, around your little finger with one sleazy smile!'

'*Sleazy?*'

'OK, charming, then, but it's the same thing. It was, in your case!'

'Gee, thanks!'

They glared at each other, and couldn't look away. Janey's skin tingled. A rather nervous-looking waiter brought them two menus and a wine list then scuttled off again, as if not wanting to risk getting caught in the crossfire. The couple at the next table—stubborn tourists who'd refused to evacuate, from the look of them—gave them an uneasy glance.

'What was the plan?' Luke murmured, still holding her gaze. He had the most gorgeous mouth, not too thin or too full, and it was almost smiling, but not quite. 'A quiet night? Some serious talking?'

Suddenly they both laughed and the tension broke.

'I guess we just needed to say it, or something,' Janey tried. Her cheeks were hot.

'Get it out of our systems.'

'Something like that…'

They looked at each other again. There was still an electric sizzle in the air that Janey could almost hear. The tiny hairs on her arms stood on end. Just the air-conditioning? Why did Luke's amber eyes look so dark, and his mouth so soft? Why had she never noticed before what a beautiful shape it was, even when he wasn't smiling?

'Can we get this clear?' he said. 'Do you still think I'm an arrogant, immature show-off, with the little-finger thing and the sleazy smile?'

'Charming,' she corrected.

'Pedantic, as usual. You said sleazy first. You said it was the same thing.'

'I don't still think it.'

'Any of it?'

'No.'

'Good.'

'How about you?'

'Do *I* think I'm an arrogant—?'

'About me. The bloody boring bit. And prim. Have to confess, I'm pretty miffed about prim.' She couldn't drag her eyes from his face, and he didn't even seem to be trying to. They'd leaned a little closer. And it was a small table. She'd be able to touch her forehead to his, two inches from now.

Oh, she couldn't keep looking at him like this!

She dropped her gaze, and so did he.

'Well, you could be prim,' he said. He spoke down to the tablecloth, low and husky, as if planning to seduce it later tonight. 'You never *were* prim, Janey, you just acted that way, and it was so damned annoying. If you'd really been prim through and through, it would have been easier because I could have thought, Oh, yeah, Alice's prim sister, and had as little to do with you as possible. But it's frustrating when you sense the diamond under the dirt and can't get to it.' He picked up his chopsticks and ran his fingers down the paper wrapper.

'Diamond. That's a lot better.'

'Listen, you're a diamond, I've always known that.' What beautiful hands he had...

'You have?' *I'm sounding breathless.*

'Underneath.'

'I guess that's why I never knew what you really thought, because the existence of any kind of *underneath* was never very apparent in you back then. You gave the impression there was just the one thin layer.'

'Well, there wasn't,' he growled. 'And there isn't now. We were both pretty young.'

'And pretty exhausted that year, working those long shifts at the hospital. I'm not sure that anyone shows their best self in those conditions. We were all snappy and short-tempered, living in each other's pockets, getting on each other's nerves.'

'Reading each other all wrong. Making so many mistakes in our personal lives because we couldn't afford to make them at work.'

'Yes. I think that's right.'

They were leaning way, *way* too close now, watching each other's hands way too intently. And neither of them was talking. The moment broke in a flash of awkwardness. He put down the chopsticks and picked up the wine list. 'Going to have wine?'

'Just a glass.'

'Red or white?'

'Shall we order first? See what goes best with what

we choose?' She looked at the menu. 'I'm thinking a nice cool dry white, because I'm going to have chilli prawns.'

'Want to share? I thought I'd go for Szechuan chicken.'

'Sounds good.'

'And Charles recommended the Peking-style vegetarian dumplings to start.'

'Yum!'

'So we agree about the food, at least.'

'I—I think we agree about a few things, Luke, we just come at them from a different angle, or something. Or we used to.'

'Maybe that's it.'

Luke looked at Janey across the table once again, wondering about the heated words that had frightened their waiter away just now. Not such a bad development, perhaps, to have argued that way. Like a shower of rain on a hot, dusty day, it had cleared the air and left something fresh and new. 'You're not married, Janey?' he asked suddenly.

She gave him a crooked smile. 'Have I mentioned a husband?'

'We haven't talked much yet.'

'Think I might have mentioned a husband.'

'OK, I guess I mean *why* aren't you married?' He knew she was more than perceptive enough to figure out his subtext—that he was actively glad she was single, so that Rowdy didn't have the complication of a stepfather figure who might not want Janey taking on a major commitment to her sister's child.

But he admitted to himself that there was something else, too. He was interested in what her unmarried status implied.

'Because for a long time I knew I wasn't ready,' she

answered. 'I didn't have a lot of confidence. Then about six years ago I thought I was. Had this horrible, needy relationship with a man—another doctor, wouldn't you know?—for three years where I did all the wrong things, and he was the wrong person anyway, and he was right to break it off in the end, but it hurt, and thank goodness I didn't slash any tyres or post diatribes on any of those don't-date-him-honey websites—'

'That's the last thing I can imagine you doing!'

'Me, too, now. But the brain had to exert firm control over the typing fingers for a couple of months there.'

'You're laughing at yourself.'

'Very healthy reaction.' She gave a dazzling grin. 'Absolute disaster to take your own broken heart too seriously. Even more of a disaster to go public about it. My advice to any woman is to make sure you surround yourself with merciless female friends who just won't let you cry and moan and rehash it over and over. *Especially* with white wine spritzers or margaritas anywhere in the picture. Ooh, yuck, no!' She wrinkled her nose, and he couldn't help laughing, which was what she wanted.

'Anyhow,' she went on, 'it was screamingly obvious that I needed some time alone, and a change of scene, so I moved to Darwin and that's been great. Just great. I learned a heck of a lot from the whole sorry episode.'

She laughed again, and Luke had this absurd flash of thought. *Then I should thank the man.* He asked instead, 'So you're settled there permanently?'

She was right on the ball. She went still and watchful at once. 'You don't want Rowdy going to Darwin, do you? So far from here, or from anywhere else you might settle?'

'No, I don't.'

'You want me to leave him here, with you.' She instantly hated the thought, he could see it.

'Not that either. Not necessarily. I want to…work something out.' It sounded inadequate. One of them would have to move, if they both wanted to take an active part in his son's future. 'Something that's best for everyone,' he finished, and this sounded more inadequate still.

'I've never said to myself that I'm permanently settled in Darwin,' she said slowly. 'I haven't bought a house. I'm renting. But I like the tropical climate there. Don't have the skin for it, but like it anyway. I love the lushness, and cool fans, and air-conditioning, and spicy food eaten outdoors, the whole complex ethnic mix of Darwin I like. And I like crocs and bird life and red desert just an hour or two away, and swimming pools and ocean, and those sudden sunsets, and the blasts of damp heat.'

'You want *me* to settle in Darwin.'

She laughed. 'No!'

'Because you're sure selling the place! Although I could point out that most of coastal north Queensland has the features you've mentioned.'

Their waiter dared a timid return, asking if they were ready to order, and by the time they'd chosen a wine and quibbled over whether the vegetarian dumplings should be steamed or fried, the subject of a compromise between Darwin and Queensland had somehow…

Well, he wasn't sure what else either of them could say at this point.

Start suggesting random cities?

Melbourne?

Both sets of grandparents were still there, but he

wasn't convinced that would be a good thing for Rowdy. Don and Pat Stafford had always treated Alice far too obviously as the favoured child, which hadn't been good for her, or for Janey. His own parents had done the opposite. They'd been incredibly suspicious of Alice. The Stafford and Bresciano in-laws had not meshed remotely well at family gatherings, and if they fought over their grandson…

No, Rowdy needed the qualities that Luke kept coming back to in Janey.

Her groundedness. Her good sense.

And she liked the tropical climate.

For some reason he couldn't get that idea out of his mind. As they waited for their meal, he kept getting pictures in his head. Janey sitting on her shady Darwin veranda at the end of a long day…

Did she even have a veranda? He didn't care about that detail.

She'd pour herself a long, cool drink and have her fans going. There'd be a slight mist of sweat across her collarbone, and she'd roll the side of the cold-drink glass across her forehead and lift her dark hair from the back of her neck. She'd blow out her cheeks, letting her tired breath drop from her lungs, and her limbs would flop all loose and relaxed as she sat on her…what? Veranda swing.

Oh, hell!

This is wrong.

He didn't understand it at all. The sensuality of the images, the tightening in his groin. He remembered the early chemistry between himself and Alice, which he hadn't thought about in years. Their wine arrived and he took refuge in pouring and tasting it. 'Nice,' he said. 'Um…'

'Why doesn't he speak, Luke?' she burst out suddenly. 'I'm not sure what we can work out about his future until he'll talk to us. And what if that takes weeks? What if we can't get him to talk until we understand why he doesn't? Does he need professional help? How do we handle that? I doubt there's a qualified child psychologist here in Crocodile Creek, and it can't just be anyone, it has to be someone really good, whom he trusts and responds to. Meanwhile, we have no idea what he thinks or feels. Or even what he'd like to be called.'

'He stopped speaking when Alice died?'

'That's what they told me at Mundarri. That he'd been very quiet while she was ill. Well, that's one of their spiritual healing practices. Silence and peace. It's not *wrong* exactly, is it? Premature babies really need it. Any ill person does. But as usual, at Mundarri they carried it to extremes. And then they said that after she died he stopped talking completely. And I don't know if we should push him, or act as if it's normal, or what.'

'Charles thinks we should just spend time with him. He suggested we take him out to Charm Island on Friday for a picnic. They had a lot less damage than on Wallaby Island, so most of the place is open. Pushing him doesn't sound right. You can tell he's not staying silent out of defiance.'

'He's not trying to punish the whole world.'

'No. It doesn't feel that way. Do you think?'

'No.' They sipped their wine, and their meal arrived. 'I like the Charm Island idea,' she went on. 'But it doesn't feel like *enough*. We go out to dinner to talk about the future, and end up reaching the momentous decision to go on a picnic.'

'I think it's all we can do.'

She flapped her hands. 'I know, I know.'

'On the plus side, we didn't fight.'

'Yes, we did!'

'Not about Rowdy.'

'No, not about him.'

'And you have no idea how good that feels, Janey. That we stayed rational. And put his needs first. And didn't use him like a weapon to hurt each other.'

Alice's ghost drifted over the table, but they looked at her, didn't talk about her, let her go.

'How long have you been in Crocodile Creek?' Janey asked, after the silence, and Luke picked up the conversational ball and ran with it, just as she'd wanted him to. They kept to light subjects for the rest of the meal, and Janey's one glass of wine began to create a pleasant softening around the edges of the atmosphere, and it was lovely.

Too lovely.

They sat over their meal for nearly two hours, and the glass of wine turned into a glass and a half. Alcohol was the worst excuse in the world. One and a half glasses of wine in two hours wouldn't have taken her over the legal limit for driving, let alone over the more personal limit for letting her barriers down.

But as they left to walk to his car, parked just around the corner, Luke linked his arm through hers and she laid her head on his shoulder for a moment, and that was all it took. She sighed. Why did he feel so good? Why did the contact feel so *necessary*? He heard the sigh and tipped his head to look at her. 'Janey?'

And then time stopped.

'I'm OK,' she murmured. 'I just...'

Have to cling to you, or my legs will give way.

Apparently she didn't need to actually say it. His

arms came around her, and she burrowed her head into the curve of his neck, drinking in the way he smelt. Oh, she wanted to taste his skin. Taste *someone*'s skin.

No.

His. Just his.

'Janey...' he said again, differently this time.

She felt his mouth pressing on her hair, finding her temple and her cheek. This was the moment when she could have turned away.

Should have.

But didn't.

Instead, she lifted her face to meet his, touching her lips clumsily to the corner of his mouth, wanting him so much she didn't care if it wasn't the best kiss in the world. She just wanted to stay here in his arms for hours, and touch and taste and feel.

'Janey...'

No. Please. No talking.

She anchored his jaw between her hands and kissed him *right* this time. Right, because he kissed her back, tightened his arms, let out a deep, groaning vibration of sound, parted his lips and drank the taste of her as if he wanted to drown in it.

They just stood there. Nothing else mattered. He tasted of spice and wine and erotic familiarity. He'd shaved for their evening out and he smelt so delicious. She couldn't put a name to the mingling of scents, but felt them cloaking her like some protective, wonderful garment that belonged to her alone.

She ran her fingers into his hair, felt the press of her breasts against his chest, and the bare length of her legs in Georgie's dress against the hard warmth of his thighs.

Her legs went weak and wobbly and that was wonderful because she could press against him more closely.

They were joined, the whole length of their bodies. Their clothing barely made a barrier. She could feel his increasing arousal and didn't try to slide away, just felt it, softened and pushed against it, letting her hips rock a little. Which made him groan against her mouth. 'Oh, Janey…'

His hands—those long-fingered surgeon's hands—slid over the fabric of her dress and cupped her bottom, anchoring her in place against his hardness. As if she'd had any intention of letting him go! His mouth had too much power. Needing air, she laid her head on his shoulder and just felt their hearts beating together. She stroked his neck and breathed him in, then he found her mouth again and she thought she'd never been kissed so deeply.

She was overwhelmed by how good this was. More than good. Inevitable. Unstoppable.

Except that you had to stop, eventually, when you were kissing each other in a public street. She felt the need building higher and harder in both of them, could see the direction it was heading.

Well, how many directions were there?

Only one, when it was this good.

But then some critical balance point in both their heads shifted at the same moment. The heat of need gave way to a cold shower of good sense. She couldn't have said which of them pulled back first, but he was the first one to speak. 'I'm sorry. I'm sorry. We can't do this, can we? We can't possibly! It's hopeless in so many ways I can't even count them. Give me a minute, then we'll drive.'

He walked awkwardly around to the driver's side of the car, and leaned his forearm on the roof, pressing his lips together and closing his eyes. 'I'm sorry,' he said again.

'No, don't. It was my fault, too.'

He hadn't unlocked the car. She stood there, waiting for him to realise, and remembered a hazy, indistinct incident from the past that she hadn't thought of in years. They'd kissed once before.

A fellow intern had thrown a party at the end of a particularly gruelling week in A and E, when Janey had seen two emergency admissions die, had sent several loudly abusive and ungrateful drug addicts back onto the streets after bringing them back from near fatal overdoses, and had treated a child permanently brain-damaged following a massive seizure.

She'd gone to a friend's house to get dressed up and they'd borrowed each other's clothes and started on the champagne before even getting to the party itself. She'd drunk too much, for once in her life, and so had Luke, and she hadn't eaten all day so the alcohol had poured into an empty stomach. The party had been crowded, a whole lot of wild, gyrating bodies dancing to music in the dark. She'd flirted and danced, cried on a friend's shoulder, made extravagant claims about never forgetting various casual friends whom she'd now totally forgotten, and she'd kissed two men that night.

One had been a guy she'd never seen before in her life, the brother of another intern. She'd fancied him rotten in her tipsy state, and he'd been ready to race off in a taxi to his place and fall into bed on the spot. He'd gone off in a huff when she'd explained woozily, no, sorry, it was just a kiss, because, sorry, she'd forgotten his name and, sorry, you really couldn't sleep with someone when you didn't know their name, right?

Why the hell not, he'd said.

She'd turned her back.

And then…memory extremely hazy here…she'd danced with Luke very late in the evening… And at some point that frantic, artificial energy—the need to *forget* the stressful week and the sense of failure by whatever means possible—had suddenly ebbed like bath water draining… She'd almost wept with exhaustion and stress…

Had found herself in his arms.

Given him her mouth.

Kiss me, Luke, I just need a kiss. Just one.

He'd kissed her back—for how long? Half a minute? Ten?—then apologised in a woolly, absent-minded way and staggered off. He'd had a rough week in A and E, too. Had worked about ninety hours. Had been thoroughly yelled at by some senior doctor, she knew, because several people had heard. She was pretty sure he'd gone home that night with someone else. Or at least had shared a taxi with the woman and been all over her in the car, receiving a warm welcome for his attentions.

He and Janey had both been as awkward as fourteen-year-olds the next day when they'd met up at work. Or maybe it had just been her, projecting her awkwardness onto him. A mumbled greeting. Palpable regret. Kissing someone you didn't even *like*! You shouldn't still be doing that at twenty-six, even when you were a stressed-out intern.

It must only have been a week or two later that Alice had come to the hospital to meet Janey for coffee, along with a whole group of other interns, including Luke, and had fallen for him on the spot.

Neither he nor Janey had ever talked about that kiss.

She devoutly hoped he didn't remember it, she told herself.

And she'd never been anywhere near that drunk before or since.

She heard an electronic whoop as he pressed the button on his keyring to unlock the car doors, and ducked thankfully into her seat. The town looked eerie as they drove home. Far too quiet. Undamaged buildings gave the illusion of normality in the moonlight, and then a sudden swathe of destruction came into sight down a side street—crumpled roofing lying on the ground, tangles of debris washed against the light poles near the river. The air smelt of rotting vegetation, and worse.

Apparently, her instinctive response to an overdose of death and destruction, whether in a hospital or the open air, was to dive straight into Luke Bresciano's arms. 'Got that out of our systems, thank goodness,' she said lightly.

'Yep. Our systems seem to have a few problems tonight.'

'There can't be that much left undealt with.'

'You wouldn't think.'

'I'm not going to…you know…turn it into a big issue. I like you. A lot more than I used to. We have too much to think about. And I think I had too much to drink.'

'It's all good, Janey,' he said gently.

But it wasn't.

Luke couldn't sleep.

A little embarrassed at having kept Janey out so late, he ushered her to her room in the doctors' house via the veranda instead of through the kitchen, which most people used for coming and going. He told her, 'I'm going to duck over to the hospital to get a report on Rowdy.'

'Can't I come, too?' Her eyes looked so huge and

shimmery in the dark, with only the blue light of the moon spilling beneath the veranda's wide eaves. The pull between them scared him. Where was it coming from? He didn't know. But he did know that he had to resist it. They both did. There was too much history, too many responsibilities.

This was Alice's sister, for heck's sake!

'I'll let you know if there've been any developments,' he told her, silently telegraphing, *Don't argue*, with every cell in her body. 'You need to rest.'

She nodded and disappeared obediently inside, and as he walked over to the hospital he thought about her getting ready for bed, images of her pulling Georgie's little sheath dress up over her head meshing with his sense memory of how she had felt in his arms, all passionate and unthinking and warm.

She'd initiated that kiss…sort of…but she hadn't been responsible for it.

Well, neither had he. Churned-up emotions could do funny things.

In the paediatric ward, Rowdy was fine. Sleeping. Shown a healthy appetite earlier in the evening. He should definitely be out of here tomorrow. But he still hadn't spoken, and Luke wasn't surprised. He'd begun to suspect there would have to be a trigger. They'd have to stumble onto the right emotion, the right moment, and it would probably be dramatic when it happened, and any more drama was surely the last thing his little guy needed in his life right now.

So what did you hope for in that situation? That he'd stay silent for weeks or months longer?

Back at the house…

Yeah.

Really couldn't sleep.

Lay there for two hours, rumpling up the bed and making it hotter and hotter with the friction of his restless body. Got up and went to the kitchen for some iced water, knowing that a part of him hoped he'd see Janey on a similar errand and they'd...

Talk.

Just talk.

It was all they could afford to do.

She was Alice's sister, and Rowdy's aunt.

But the kitchen was silent, as was the entire house, so he crept back to bed and tried again. Must have dozed a bit, but still felt restless and edgy and unrefreshed when dawn began to filter in through the curtains he hadn't bothered to close. He got up, put on shorts and a T-shirt and went out to finish cleaning the pool.

'You've done an incredible job with the pool, Luke!' Georgie exclaimed over breakfast. 'Is it swimmable yet?'

'Probably need to give it another few hours for the chemicals to settle.'

'Did you see it, Janey?' Georgie asked.

'Not yet.'

'She helped yesterday,' Luke said, although he was giving her too much credit.

'You wouldn't let me help, Luke!' she protested. 'I wiped down a couple of chairs.'

Half of Crocodile Creek's medical personnel seemed to have converged on the kitchen for breakfast this morning. Janey's head began to spin from the overlapping conversations, the belated introductions, the new, curious faces, and she couldn't eat. The whole-grain cereal went gluggy in her bowl and the coffee tasted too bitter and strong. She hadn't slept well last night, and Luke didn't look as if he had either.

She'd begun to regret their kiss as soon as it had ended but in the bright light of day it seemed like not just a minor glitch, like that other kiss they'd shared eight years ago, but a huge, glaring misjudgement. He'd once been her sister's husband. *Nobody* needed this kind of complication, not Rowdy, not Luke, not she herself.

Cal Jamieson came in, following an overnight stint in A and E. 'Who did the pool? It's sparkling.'

'Luke,' said Georgie. 'Doesn't it look great?'

Cal clapped him on the back. 'Good on you! The kids can swim after school. Now, if you want to help the clean-up team with the mess on the beach…'

'Give him a break!' Georgie protested. 'He must have been out there before dawn.'

They all seemed unreasonably impressed by Luke's hard work, and made a big deal of it the way a parent might if a surly and unhelpful teen suddenly turned around and washed the dinner dishes without being asked. Janey wondered about it. He surely couldn't have acquired a reputation as a shirker. However shallow and ego-driven she might have thought him eight years ago, she would never have accused him of slacking off where work was concerned. It was something else that had impressed them.

'How's Rowdy?' someone asked.

'You know, that's going to be his name for ever, unless he protests,' said someone else. Janey was losing track of who was who.

'Is that OK, Luke?' Georgie frowned. 'We kind of…saddled him with it in a fit of frustration, because we had to call him something, but it's up to you.'

Luke gave a slow, reluctant smile. 'I'm good with Rowdy. If he is. He responds to it, at least.'

'I think he responds mainly to the sound of someone opening the fridge door.'

They all laughed, but then the atmosphere went a little cautious and quiet. Not Alice's ghost this time, but an awareness in all of them that for Rowdy/Felixx/Frankie Jay there was still a long way to go.

Three doctors OK'd his discharge later that morning. Hospital caretaker and handyman Walter Grubb came and inspected Luke's work with the pool. He tested the water and pronounced it safe for human immersion, someone rustled up a pair of boy's swim shorts that more or less fitted, and Janey and Rowdy went swimming.

They had the loveliest, laziest day, while Luke did a long shift at the hospital. Between swims, they lolled by the pool in the shade, sucking on icy poles or drinking fresh fruit smoothies that were thick with crushed ice, yoghurt and full-cream milk, and tasted of the very expensive peaches and strawberries and bananas that were now being trucked in to the stricken region on the damaged roads.

Rowdy could swim like a frog, and he was a joy to behold, wriggling down to the bottom of the pool and back up again, doing cannonballs and twists off the side. He tired himself out by two o'clock and Janey insisted on a nap, giving him the double bed she was using because it had a ceiling fan above it, which made the room cooler.

He went out like a light and she sat on the side of the bed and watched him, then felt so sleepy herself that she lay down beside him, thinking she'd just close her eyes for a minute or two…or five…and enjoy the precious, peaceful sound of him breathing.

So much for that plan. She fell asleep herself, and neither of them stirred for two hours.

Another long swim soon freshened them up and then the house started filling again towards the end of the day. Georgie brought Max and CJ home from school. CJ belonged to Gina and Cal, Janey had discovered. Charles dropped in to see how Rowdy was doing. Someone suggested a sausage sizzle beside the pool to celebrate its return to active service.

Janey was amazed and impressed at the way everyone took up the idea and got into action. Mrs Grubb answered the appeal for salad ingredients, and promised her potato salad, still warm, with mustard dressing, in less than an hour, but the medical staff did most of the preparation themselves.

The division of labour fell along gender lines. The women rushed around the kitchen, slicing onions, grating carrot, cooking tortellini, their conversation pitched at a level of urgency Janey would have expected during emergency surgery.

'Wait! Don't put the tortellini in until I find the jar of pesto sauce, because maybe there isn't any!'

'I don't think we need watermelon salad as well, if we've got the tortellini and pesto…'

'Where are the cherry tomatoes?'

'*And* the carrot and raisin salad, too. It's too much.'

'It's fine. There's a ton of fresh mint growing around the bottom of the steps, we should use it. And how many are we, anyway? Has anyone counted?'

Janey just kept her head down and did what she was told with a knife and a chopping board. She liked the lively atmosphere, but was content to be more of a spectator than a participant. What would it be like to live and work here? she wondered.

Someone exclaimed again about Luke cleaning the pool. 'It's the first time he's really got involved in something outside the hospital.'

'Your influence, Janey?' someone else suggested.

'No,' she said at once. 'It's because he's found his son.' And the women all nodded and murmured, conceding that she was right.

Meanwhile, the men performed primal male rituals with the barbecue grill, about ten kilos of sausages and some lethal-looking stainless-steel forks and tongs. There was a brief panic over tomato ketchup, but somebody found it. Several kids, dripping with pool water, announced that they were *starving*. It was dark by this time, but the air was still steamy and warm, and someone had set up outdoor lights and mosquito coils to keep the bugs away.

Everything smelt fabulous. The salads and cups and dishes and cutlery were ferried out to the poolside to the big picnic table that had been brought out from under the veranda. The sausages were pronounced ready. The kids ate them slathered with fried onion and ketchup, wrapped in bread slices, and flavoured slightly with chlorine from their wet fingers.

The adults piled their paper plates with salads as well as the sausages and onions, and ate while watching the kids when they went back in the pool. Somebody set up the CD player on the veranda and put on some rock and roll.

Sitting at the foot of her favourite lounging chair, Janey watched Luke finish loading his plate and come over to sit beside her.

'The best get-togethers at Crocodile Creek are always the ones with no preparation,' he said.

'You can take most of the credit for this one, Luke,' she answered. 'If you hadn't cleaned the pool, this wouldn't be happening.'

He shrugged. 'It's Grubby's job, but I knew he wouldn't get to it for days because there's so much else that has a higher priority at the moment.'

'You've impressed everyone, I think.'

'I've kept to myself a bit around here. Maybe they didn't think I had that much community spirit.'

She sensed that he was playing down the change in his own outlook, so she didn't push the subject, saying instead, 'Look at Rowdy.'

'I know.'

They watched him as they ate. Max and CJ were having a jumping-into-the-pool competition, with Alistair and Cal acting as judges. They gave points for style and splash.

Rowdy had shaken his head when asked if he wanted to compete, but he took part on the sidelines, waiting until the other two boys had completed each jump then trying ambitious imitations of his own. Cal and Alistair were both great about it, issuing the right *wow* sounds at regular intervals and applauding his most impressives splashes.

'He's a good swimmer,' Janey said.

'He seems to love it.'

'I just can't think of Mundarri as paradise, but he must have had some wonderful times up there. They had a waterfall with a natural pool at the base of it. Pristine and deep and clear, with a bed of pebbles. He learned to swim in that, they told me. He made dams and channels and pebble castles.'

'Sounds great.'

'It was.' She made a face at him. 'If you don't mind getting a few leeches.'

'City kids can be too squeamish about things like that. Look at him now!'

'Rowdy! Gold-medal twister bomb there, mate!' Joe exclaimed. He'd left Christina's hospital bedside to come and eat, looking tired but content. Little Isabella Jane was in perfect health, he'd reported, and she was a natural at breast-feeding. Christina still felt pretty sore, but had insisted she'd be well enough to leave the hospital in time to get to Cal and Gina's beach wedding in two days' time, if someone could push a wheelchair onto the sand.

'Dynamite!' Cal agreed.

Rowdy pulled himself out of the pool, streaming with water, hair plastered down on his head, grinning from ear to ear. He looked around for Max, as if wanting to make sure Max had seen the twister bomb, too. He took in a giant breath and opened his mouth. Janey clutched Luke's arm.

'He's going to speak! He's going to yell for Max to watch him. He…' She stopped.

Rowdy seemed to freeze where he stood. His wet hands clapped over his mouth and he seemed stricken and terrified out of nowhere. Cal, Gina and Alistair were all watching him as he stood there still streaming wet, looking suddenly so thin and small and alone in the middle of the barbecue crowd. Max and CJ took no notice of what was happening. Most of the adults were talking and hadn't stopped to watch three little boys playing an ordinary water game.

'Watch this one, CJ!' Max said.

'No, let's do it together!' Both boys made enormous leaps into the water.

'What's wrong with him?' Janey murmured. She made a move to get up and go to Rowdy, but Luke held her back with a hand planted on her shoulder, which meant they were both holding onto each other now, because for some reason she hadn't yet let go of his arm. 'Luke?'

'Let's give him a minute. I'm not sure what's happening.'

'I just want to hold him. He's upset.'

'But what's going on in that little head? If we watch, maybe we can work something out.'

So she sat back down and they watched, half-expecting that he'd forget whatever had troubled him and would be back in the water in another few seconds.

But he didn't forget. He crept forlornly over to the remaining piece of fence, where he'd hung his towel. He wrapped it around himself and began to pick his way towards the house in his bare feet. He gave off the impression that he was sending himself into exile.

CHAPTER SIX

'I WANT to go after him,' Janey said.

'No.' Luke still wouldn't let her move.

She made another attempt to shake him off, but he only slid his arm around to her other shoulder and held her more firmly where she sat. He felt warm and strong, and she was very glad he was there, very glad they didn't drive each other crazy any more.

Far too glad, probably. Their blossoming connection was undeniably powerful, because it concerned a child who was linked to each of them by blood and heart and history, and whom they both cared so much about. But Luke Bresciano was Alice's ex-husband, and that made it feel wrong. He'd loved Alice first.

She had to shake off this aching need.

'I'm thinking, Janey,' he said, sounding as tense as she felt. 'I looked up some stuff at the hospital today about mute children and post-traumatic stress disorder, but it didn't seem to fit.'

'In what way?'

'It's depressive mostly in those kinds of cases. It's associated with generalised apathy and night terrors, and it often comes on gradually. I don't know. Maybe it's pointless trying to work this out.'

'I want to hear it, Luke.'

'A lot of the stuff I found related to refugee children in detention centres. It's horrible and this country needs to make some big changes in how it handles those cases, but it just didn't seem relevant to Rowdy. He wanted to speak just now.'

'Yes, desperately. You could see it, feel it. I really thought he would.'

'You're right, he was on the point of it, and it was probably to get CJ and Max's attention, to say, "Watch this!" just the way the two bigger boys are doing with each other.'

'But then he stopped himself.'

'Exactly. Because he remembered that he wasn't *allowed* to. But why does he think he's not allowed to?' His thigh pressed against hers and she let the contact stay, despite all her reluctance and doubt. 'What does he think is going to happen if he does?'

'I don't know. I have no idea.'

'Surely we've all made it clear to him that he's welcome and wanted and loved and has the right to say anything he wants!'

'I've tried. And I've tried not to scare him with too much at once. Kids don't always need high emotion.'

'Georgie reminded me of that. Just to take it moment by moment, just to do the ordinary things together. And yet he seemed terrified.'

'I want to go and find him. He's disappeared into the house and I need to know that he's safe, Luke.' She gripped his hand, and then his strong wrists. 'That he won't just let himself out of another door onto the far veranda, wander down the steps and disappear.'

'Yes. All right.' He squeezed her shoulders again,

then they both stood. He ran his hand down her bare arm as if he didn't want to let her go, and she felt the same. No matter how hard she tried to keep rational about this, keep a safe cushion of distance, fight its deeper implications, she felt so close to him, linked by what they both felt for Rowdy and utterly safe in sharing all her fears. She belonged by his side, at least when they were following his son.

'Situation in hand?' Alistair asked as they went past him. Gina and Cal were still covertly watching, and Janey caught glances from a couple of others also.

'Leave it to us,' Luke answered. 'Whatever's going on, he doesn't need a crowd.'

They found him easily enough—in the kitchen, eating the leftover cubes of watermelon that hadn't been used in the watermelon salad. He looked up at the sound of the screen door opening, then turned away deliberately, as if it wasn't even safe to look at them.

Because then he might be tricked out of his self-imposed silence?

'Sweetheart, what's wrong?' Janey asked, coming close.

Nothing.

Luke pulled out a kitchen chair and sat in it back to front, leaning his forearms over the chair back and hunching down so he was almost at eye level with Rowdy. In the one light that someone had left on above the stove, his dark hair gleamed and his tanned arms looked like dusty teak.

'Listen, little mate,' he said, 'something is making you scared to talk, and we want to help. People need to talk, you know. That's how we understand each other, and we want to understand you. We really do. It's not wrong. If someone's told you that something bad is going to happen if you talk... That's wrong, OK? That's not true.'

He waited.

Silence.

'Luke's right, sweetheart,' Janey said. 'Nothing bad is going to happen if you talk.'

But he said nothing, and he didn't look as if he believed them. Still frozen to the spot, so little and tightly held in, he blinked, squeezing his eyes shut until moisture appeared at the corners. That struggle was still going on inside him. Should they push? Should they try to get him over that edge of control somehow? *Make* him speak?

But it was getting late. She looked at Luke and they reached a silent agreement not to push him any more tonight. They still didn't understand enough about what was going on. 'For now?' he murmured.

'Yes.'

They gave each other a wry smile. At least their communication with each other was working, and that was worth a lot.

'Bedtime,' Luke announced. 'How about another Thomas the Tank story?'

Rowdy nodded. He wasn't yet ready to smile.

'Teeth first,' Janey said. 'And a good night's sleep because we're going on that picnic tomorrow, remember?'

He nodded again. Still no smile.

Twenty minutes later, Janey put on the electric jug for a cup of tea and Luke came back from Rowdy's bedroom to report, 'Almost asleep before the end of the story. I think he's exhausting himself with whatever's going on inside him. It's not just the physical effect of everything he's been through. What time did he wake up this morning?'

'Eight-thirty.'

'And he had a two-hour nap, and now it's only eight-fifteen.'

'I know. But maybe lots of sleep is the best thing for him.'

'I think so. I think we just have to let all of this go at its own pace. Have to tell you, it's very good that you and I are not at odds over this. A huge plus.'

'I think so, too. Do you want tea?' The electric jug had begun to sing.

Luke glanced out the kitchen window in the direction of the pool. 'People are still in the water, and a few have headed back to the hospital. It's much quieter in here, isn't it? Yes, let's sit for a while.'

Janey poured the tea and they both sat at the kitchen table, sharing many of the same thoughts, no doubt, but not many words. The refrigerator hummed. Laughter and conversation drifted up from beside the pool. The peace in here wouldn't last. Soon, people would start bringing in the leftovers and the dirty dishes. CJ and Max would be ready for bed, too. But for now...

'I'm trying to think how it would have been if I hadn't found your address amongst Alice's things,' Janey said.

He took in a quick breath. 'Don't.'

'No, I know, it's too hard to contemplate.'

'Those maybes and what-ifs. I used to torture myself with them in London after Alice disappeared with him. You can't think about the what-ifs.'

'But I wanted to tell you that I'm glad I brought him here. Because it means there's someone else who cares about him in the same way I do, and that's so good.'

'Yes. It is.'

'I—I really need it, Luke. Whatever happens, I want

you to know that I'm not going to be heading out of here
on the next plane. I'm giving this some time.'

'I appreciate it. You always were...' He paused and
fished around for a word. Came up with 'sensible.'

She made a face. 'Gee, thanks!'

He threw back his head and laughed, something he
hadn't done very often over the past two days. 'Want to
give me another shot at that?'

'Not sure I'm prepared to take that much of a risk.'

'You're good, Janey, OK? You've been bloody
great every single minute since our first talk on
Tuesday afternoon...'

'Our first fight, you mean.'

'I like fighting with you. It clears the air. And I need
you every bit as much as you need me.'

They looked at each other over their mugs of
steaming tea and teetered on the edge of saying more.
Or doing more. The fridge stopped humming. Janey
heard someone call out, 'Bring in the bread.'

Good. They'd be interrupted any second. It was the
only thing that would save her from doing something
really, really impossible and dumb with the man her
sister had been so cruel to.

But even the interruption didn't save her in the end,
because when most people had gone to bed a couple of
hours later, and Janey herself couldn't sleep, she went
along to Rowdy's room to check on him and there was
Luke, in a white T-shirt and a pair of dark blue cotton
boxer shorts, doing the same thing.

Rowdy was breathing peacefullly beneath his light
cotton sheet, lying on his back with his head turned to
one side. It was a trusting position and he looked so

relaxed and still, his skin as tender as a baby's and his lashes dark on his cheeks.

He didn't need anything right now.

'But how about you?' Luke asked Janey softly. Now they stood just outside Rowdy's door. It was the right moment to wish each other good night and just...just *leave*, head in opposite directions down the corridor. It shouldn't be so hard!

'I'm not expecting to sleep for a while,' she said. 'I had that big nap this afternoon, just like Rowdy did.'

'Want to go for a walk or something?' He shifted, and a floorboard creaked.

'In bare feet and my nightie?' Which had been in the overnight bag that had survived the bus crash, and was just a short, strappy bit of blue, lace-edged silk that kept her cool during Darwin's hot nights.

'I'll lend you a T-shirt to put over it, and some thongs. Come on. I can't stay in the house.'

'All right.' His almost impatient assumption that she would join him drew her in.

He wasn't being arrogant or pushy, he was just, oh, *counting* on her.

Trusting her.

Acknowledging this strong, rock-solid foundation they both seemed to be standing on together. She somehow knew that if she'd spoken the same words to him—*Come on, I can't stay in the house*—he would have responded with the same agreement.

She followed him to his room and stood inside the doorway, watching him dig through his T-shirt drawer in the dark, because he hadn't wanted to blind both of them with a sudden flood of light. 'This one's pretty new.' He held it out.

'Because I couldn't possibly wear one of your old T-shirts, could I?' She stepped further into the room and took it from him. 'Yuck! They must be disgusting!' She realised too late how flirty she sounded, teasing him like that.

His body went still as she took the shirt, and he didn't let it go. 'Don't tease me,' he said.

'I'm sorry…'

'No, damn it, do tease me! Do anything you want with me!' He pulled suddenly on the T-shirt, reeling her close. 'I don't care, I just…' He didn't bother to finish. His body said the words instead.

Want you.

And he knew she felt the same. He had to know. The same strength. The same rightness. Everything.

He bent and rolled his forehead across hers, dropped the T-shirt, curved his palms over her bare shoulders, bent lower and kissed her collarbone and her neck, and then the slope of one breast where the lace ended. She stood motionless and let her eyes drift shut, pretending to herself for one more moment that this wasn't her decision, that it was all coming from him.

But it wasn't. It was in her just as much. All through her.

She lifted her face in search of a kiss and felt the light brush of his mouth against her parted lips. He took it achingly slowly and sweetly, still holding her shoulders with his warm hands, tasting her lightly and then going deeper, making her lips part further to receive him, drawing her tongue into a dance.

He stepped close against her, and she discovered how aroused he was. Mmm. Oh. Delicious. She grabbed his hips and pulled him as close as he could get, and he wrapped his arms hard around her, then ran his hands everywhere. Down her back. Into the soft creases at the tops of her thighs. Over her tingling breasts.

He slid the straps off her shoulders, and kissed his way down to one nipple and then the other, and that was fine, it was perfect. Oh, it was so good, it made her gasp. He lavished her breasts with the touch of his mouth, ran the tip of his tongue around her nipples, cupped her and buried his face in the valley he'd made.

'You have such a beautiful body…'

'So do you. I want you *so much*.' She curled her fingers in his dark hair, needing him to anchor her in a universe that had become unsteady down to its very foundations. She twisted her head back, breathless and desperate for more.

There was too much fabric in the way. She lifted the hem of his T-shirt and helped him pull it over his head, and then her silk slip slid down between their bodies and pooled around her feet, and all there was left was skin.

Skin and a fairly ineffective pair of boxer shorts, which he soon got rid of. They came together again and he felt like warm satin against her breasts and her stomach and her legs. Holding her upper thighs, he lifted her and she wrapped her legs around him while he carried her to the bed.

'Do you want this?' he demanded.

'Yes.'

'Are you using birth control?'

'No…'

'Then I will.'

But he kissed her first, kneeling beside the bed and reaching for her, kissing her everywhere, *everywhere*, bringing her gasping to the brink, so that she began to beg him, 'Don't stop yet. Not yet.'

'Ten seconds. I have to.'

'Yes. OK. Yes.'

And then he was inside her, with one effortless thrust. She held him, pushed her hips against him and drew them back, bringing them closer, bringing him deeper. He rolled, sliding her whole body on top of his, and buried his face between her breasts again, tightened his arms around her and rocked.

The world exploded, a shattering of stars behind her closed lids, panting breath. They squeezed each other and clung and she heard a groan tear from his body, while she was almost sobbing with the power of her release.

When she laid her head against his chest a few moments later, she heard his heart pounding, and could have stayed in his arms listening to it all night. All night, tomorrow night, for ever.

'Janey...' he said, after a few minutes.

'I'm still here.'

'I know you are. Happy?'

'Yes.' She slid to lie beside him, and he tangled his legs with hers and rested a hand on her breast.

'I wish you could stay all night,' he said.

'Me, too.' She thought about it for a moment. 'I guess I can't. Rowdy might come looking for me.'

And if he found her in the wrong bed, with Luke, he wouldn't even be able to ask the funny little five-year-old questions that would give them their cue for tackling the subject in the right way. She didn't want Rowdy finding her in Luke's bed.

Not yet.

'We probably—' he began.

'Don't say that it shouldn't have happened,' she cut in. It might be true, but she didn't want to hear it. Didn't want him to spell it out for her, speaking gently in case she didn't realise.

She did realise.

She knew it shouldn't have happened. She also knew she'd be feeling just as restless and confused and full of questions if she'd managed to stay safely in her own bed. Was he looking for Alice? It hadn't felt that way just now. All those times over the past couple of days when she'd felt as if Alice's ghost had been hovering between them... Alice's ghost hadn't been here tonight, not for a second.

And what am I looking for?

If she gave Luke her heart, and found he didn't want it because when he came to his senses he realised that he'd done this for one great big wrong reason, what would she do?

Learn to live with her heart shattered in pieces.

The idea frightened her.

'We kissed once before, do you remember?' she heard herself asking him, and didn't know why she'd said it.

He shifted and laughed, kissed her shoulder. 'As it was only last night, yes!'

'No. I don't mean last night. Hope you'd remember that! Before. Way before. Eight years ago.'

'What?'

'Yeah, it was at a party and we'd had too much to drink. We'd both had a rotten week in A and E. Heroin addicts and yelling doctors, and patients we couldn't save. So we all gathered at someone's place to let off some steam.'

'Not ringing any bells yet, Janey.'

She pushed on, still not knowing why. 'And I was crying on my friends' shoulders, saying all sorts of ex-

travagant things, and you were, oh, chatting up every
woman in sight and showing off as usual—'

'And this is your idea of the right conversation topic
for an interlude like this.'

'I want to say it, Luke.'

'Apparently. Have I any power to stop you?' He
squeezed her, to soften the words.

'And I kissed this bloke I didn't even know.' She
knew she was testing Luke's patience now, but for some
reason this was important. 'And he wanted to race off
to his place, but I said, no, and then I just, basically, fell
on you and locked lips.'

'Sounds like a great kiss!'

'To be honest, I can't remember if it was.'

'I don't believe it really happened.'

'It did. It probably only lasted a few seconds. I don't
think it was your first kiss of the evening, or your last.
I'm not surprised you don't remember.'

'So why are we talking about it?'

'I just wondered, that's all.'

'Wondered what?'

'If any of it had stuck. I hadn't thought about it
myself for years, and then last night I did. But it didn't
trigger the same memory for you. And I just wondered.'

'You're spoiling something that doesn't need to be
spoiled, Janey. Spoiling something wonderful that I
won't forget. Can you stop?'

He was right. She'd known it even while she'd been
saying it, but it was hard to be wise when your whole
life had just been shaken into pieces by one man's touch.

They caught the nine-thirty boat out to Charm Island the
next morning. Liberally coated in sunscreen and wear-

ing a broad-brimmed canvas hat, Rowdy hung on the rail for the whole journey, seeming captivated by the sight of the water. He'd probably never been out on the ocean before, and might not even remember having seen the sea.

It was too soon to gauge what Cyclone Willie had done to the Barrier Reef itself, as they passed the halfway point of the one-hour trip. Skirting several kilometres to the south of Wallaby Island, which was much larger as well as closer to the mainland, they could see how much more extensive the damage must have been there. The island's rugged skyline looked like a torn sheet of paper, with so much vegetation shredded and destroyed. Charm Island had fallen just beyond the outer edge of the worst damage.

Some people were making dire predictions about the future of tourism and the Reef in this area. Others said that the marine life and the coral itself would fare well, and the focus of environmental concern needed to be the tracts of rainforest in the path of the cyclone after it had hit the coast.

The resort at Charm Island's southern end looked messy but its infrastructure was basically intact. As the boat approached the jetty, in the sheltered waters of a curving bay, Luke and Janey saw a row of roofless cabins fronting the water and a litter of trees and branches on the ground, but a second row of cabins further back towards the island's forested slopes still had bright beach towels hanging on their wooden deck railings and groupings of outdoor chairs.

On shore, a signpost and map board indicated various activities. The animal park and windsurfing were listed as closed, and they could see the torn netting and broken supports of what must have been an impressive aviary, but various other sport and water activities and two of the three nature trails that led into the rugged interior of the island were open.

'Play on the beach?' Luke suggested, and that seemed fine with Rowdy.

They spent two hours on the sand, digging holes and making castles in between taking refreshing dips in water that had settled back to its brilliant tropical colour instead of its recent stormy brown. Then they explored the resort buildings and at the gift shop Janey bought Rowdy a stained-glass kit which he could make up into a circular picture of tropical coral and fish.

He looked pleased about it and wanted to carry it himself, but she told him, 'We'd better keep it in the day pack. Wouldn't be good if you dropped it or forgot it somewhere.' He gave a silent nod.

In the end they'd decided not to bring a picnic, because the mere mention of one had thrown Mrs Grubb into such a flap—she'd apparently pictured goat cheese tartlets and smoked salmon croquettes, even though they'd insisted salad sandwiches would be fine. She had enough in the catering department to worry about at the moment, so they'd told her, 'We'll buy lunch there.'

There was a buffet on offer in the resort's biggest restaurant. Rowdy piled his plate high, trying everything from crab claws to sliced roast beef to peppers stuffed with spicy rice.

Luke ruffled his hair. 'You are a brilliant eater, kid!' He didn't let the physical contact linger. He had to hold himself back sometimes, Janey could see. Had to force himself to show less than he felt. They hadn't even begun to talk about how or when to tell Rowdy that this man was his dad.

And they hadn't talked about last night, which repeated itself over and over in her mind. It ambushed her whenever she looked at him and so did the knowledge that it might never be repeated.

After the big meal, Rowdy looked a little sleepy, so they found a shady place beside the kids' playground. The shade sail above the play equipment had survived the cyclone—probably by being taken down and stored away. It stretched above them, a cool jade green, offering relief from the midday heat of the sun. Rowdy played on the equipment for a while, then came and lay down on his towel at Janey's suggestion and slept.

'He seems good today,' Luke murmured, watching him.

'Maybe it's easier for him, in some ways, when Max and CJ aren't around, even though they're building a nice friendship, the three of them. But when it's just us, he doesn't have to keep such a close watch on himself, doesn't have to keep reminding himself not to talk. There's not the same exuberance.' Janey rolled onto her stomach and propped herself on her elbows, so she could look at Luke as she talked to him.

Luke wished she hadn't.

Or he wished that Georgie had a different preference in swimsuit styles.

This was Alice's sister, and it disturbed him, this new awareness of her and need for her as a woman. It irritated him, disturbed him, confused him, made him restless and unsure. He knew he shouldn't have given in to it last night, but even in hindsight couldn't pinpoint the moment where he should have or could have turned away.

The whole thing played in his head like a loop of

videotape, only that wasn't quite right, because there was so much more to it than mere sight and sound. The feel of her skin. The taste of her. The trust in the whole length of her body when she pressed against him.

And there'd been no games.

However right or wrong or just plain crazy it had been for them to pull each other's clothes off and explode in each other's arms, there had been no games. She'd kissed him because she felt the same need that he did. She'd given in to their blazing desire because, as had happened to him, it had taken control of her whole being and she hadn't been able to think straight.

Then they'd both come back to earth and had that weird, awkward and unsettling conversation about having kissed before. Why had she asked him about that? He had no idea.

But at no point had she pretended to feel more than she did, in order to see how much passion or vulnerability he might betray.

Alice had been the Stafford sister who'd played games.

These comparisons—they unnerved him. The idea that he'd kissed Janey eight years ago unnerved him, too. It must have been very dark, very late, and she'd said they'd both had too much to drink. Was it possible he hadn't even realised who she was? He tried to think. What might she have been wearing? No, it wasn't going to come back to him. It had totally gone.

'How long since you spoke to your parents?' he asked quickly, to distract himself.

'Wednesday.'

'Have you mentioned me?'

'Not yet. We should have talked about this before, I suppose.'

'There's too much to talk about, all of it sensitive. It's fine. I think it was the right decision not to tell them yet.'

'I'm making all my decisions on the run, it feels. And I haven't told them that he's not speaking. They're...pretty fragile right now, especially my mother. My aunt is staying with them, helping them through, which is what gives me the freedom to take things slowly with Rowdy.'

'So what do they think? Why do they think you're in Crocodile Creek?'

'I told them I took the bus to the coast so we could fly out from a bigger airport.' She gave a self-mocking shudder. 'Which is not so far from the truth, because I am not a big fan of outback mail-hop flights!'

He laughed and asked, 'Have you travelled much?'

'Been out of Australia twice. Once to New Zealand, once to Bali. I'm not exactly an intrepid world explorer.'

'Some people would consider practising medicine in a place like Darwin to be intrepid enough.'

'There are some challenges,' she agreed.

They talked like this until Rowdy woke up. Lazy and easy, punctuated with gulps of iced water from the day pack they'd brought, no mention of last night. He could see that she was thinking about it sometimes, though, the way he was. Just the way she moved a shoulder, or looked away. A self-consciousness in her smile, and a sudden bloom of colour in her cheeks.

He wanted to tell her, *It's OK. We're OK.*

But he didn't know if it was true. Maybe something delicate and precious had been ruined.

Rowdy was thirsty after he'd stretched and blinked and rubbed his eyes. He took a long drink from his water bottle, and then Luke suggested, 'How about one of those nature trails? I'd be interested to see more of the island, the damage and what's still intact. It's only three o'clock.'

'Do we want to take the boat that leaves at five?' Janey asked.

'There are only two more after that, on the hour at six and seven, and those both seem a bit late.'

'Suit you, Rowdy? A bit of an explore, and then the five o'clock boat?'

He nodded and scrambled to his feet, while Luke and Janey put T-shirts and shorts back on over their swim-suits. He was a pretty impressive hiker, it turned out. By the time they passed the helipad and then the extensively damaged aviary and animal enclosures he was a good fifty metres ahead of them. He covered the ground like an eager puppy, running until he was almost out of sight, then he stopped to examine something that had caught his interest, and circled back to hold out a shiny dead beetle for their inspection.

The beetle was iridescent and beautiful, all greeny gold like shot silk, and Janey exclaimed over it with sincere interest, earning his rare grin. 'Want to keep it and bring it home to show Max and CJ?'

He nodded, and she wrapped it in a clean tissue and put it in the side pocket of their day pack.

'No sign of any animals or birds in these enclosures,' Janey said when he'd run off ahead again.

'They must have lost a few, especially the birds.' Luke peered into the damaged aviary. 'But I heard one of the staff in the gift shop say that they've got tempo-rary accommodation set up somewhere for the survi-vors. Their animal collection can't have been that extensive, just a few cute marsupials for the overseas tourists. I think the birds were the main focus.'

Beyond the aviary, the island quickly lost its resort flavour and became a wilderness of hoop pine, eucalyptus trees and lush pockets of thick rainforest. Their hiking trail meandered in the cool shade, skirting the surprisingly steep heights of the interior. They passed a couple of families on their way back to the resort, but otherwise the trail remained quiet and peaceful.

'I don't like it when we lose sight of him,' Janey said.

'I'm sure he feels very safe here. He's used to country much wilder than this.'

'That doesn't mean he is safe.'

'Janey, I understand why you're nervous—'

'I know. I'm being over-protective. But he's still only five. He's been through so much.'

This time Luke didn't argue, just put his arm around her shoulder and squeezed her, kissed the top of her head. She smelt the hot cotton of his shirt and just wanted to lay her head against him and surrender all control.

What's happening?

They were so comfortable together, even with all those unanswered questions about last night. She hadn't known it was possible to feel so trusting and so on edge at the same time. He let her go without holding the moment of contact, but the pull between them lingered in the air like a delectable scent, and she knew she wanted much more.

She wanted them to make love again. He did, too, she was sure. The awareness and the complexity made her dizzy. Giddy with wanting. Woozy from the vertigo brought on but so many unanswered questions.

The rational part of her mind couldn't trust that what she felt was anything more than the relief of having his rock-like support and knowing he felt the same as she did about Rowdy.

Yes, the rational part, but, oh, the intuition…!

The thing was, she'd never trusted intuition. That particular rug could get pulled from under your feet so fast that your self-esteem ended up flat on the floor. She wouldn't give in to it again. Not with so much still unresolved. Not when this was Alice's ex.

Setting her jaw, she eased away from him on the path. It was wide enough. They didn't need to walk this close together. Behind them, she heard thudding footsteps and two boys darted through the space she'd just opened up between herself and Luke. They ran and laughed, jostling each other, fighting a bit. They looked like brothers, one around eleven and the other a couple of years younger.

The younger one's laughter turned to a whine as he struggled to keep up. 'Wait, Sam! I said it wasn't a race.' His big brother elbowed him, playful but too rough, pushing him against the bushes at the side of the path. 'I'll tell Mum you're being mean,' he whined again.

'Oh, come on, Josh, don't be a baby…'

They disappeared around a bend in the trail. It must have been less than a minute later that Janey and Luke heard a boy's voice again, but this time it sounded very different.

Urgent.

Angry.

And several years younger.

'Back away! Leave it alone or it'll go for you! It's hurt. Stay quiet and steady and back away! Back *away*!'

'That's not those two kids who just went past,' Luke said slowly. 'Whose is that voice?'

He moved at once into a loping run and Janey followed just behind him. He wore rubber-soled athletic shoes while she had on flat sandals, which she cursed as she struggled to keep up and got dirt scuffed in through the open toes. They rounded the bend almost sprinting and there was Rowdy.

Yelling.

CHAPTER SEVEN

'It'll kick! Back away!' Rowdy yelled.

Fifty metres ahead stood the two brothers and in front of them, right on the trail, was a cassowary nearly two metres tall. It was a beautiful creature, a powerfully built, flightless bird with coarse, heavy feathers in a gorgeous, shimmering arrangement of purple and dark blue, offset by a drape of orange-red around the neck like a scarf, and a dark, keel-shaped crest on the top of its head.

'It's hurt!' Rowdy yelled. His face was red and screwed up tight in his frustration. He bent low and loped forward as he spoke, as if believing that he needed to be closer to get his urgent message across. He was trying to yell and keep his voice to a whisper at the same time, trying to make himself as unobtrusive as possible, so that he didn't aggravate the cassowary even more. 'Can't you see? It'll go for you!'

It did.

The boys had ignored all Rowdy's frantic warnings. Was the older one trying to protect his younger brother? Did they both think that it was safe to taunt the creature? Or were they simply too frozen in fear to make any response at all? Janey and Luke had no time to tell, and they were still too far away to help. Luke bent down, grabbed a stick and ran, but it was no use.

When a cassowary felt threatened, it attacked.

The bird darted forward heavily, limping from its wound and yet still powerful on its strong legs. It kicked at the older boy.

Once.

Twice.

And again.

Fast, frightening, incredibly vicious thrusts.

The boy was on the ground, screaming. Even from this distance Janey could see the blood. Arterial blood. There was no mistaking that dark spurting from high on his inner thigh. Luke had charged at the bird, yelling at the top of his lungs and waving the stick, and whether it was the noise or his size or the fact that the beautiful creature had given itself a fresh burst of pain with those kicks from its wounded leg, it was enough.

The cassowary fled into the bush, and Janey was amazed at how silently it managed to move through the dense undergrowth, and how quickly it was lost to sight. Within seconds, it had disappeared.

Janey reached Rowdy and gave him a quick, fierce hug, feeling that awful, guilty wash of relief that *her* child was safe, even though someone else's wasn't. She'd seen it in parents in hospital emergency rooms, and now she understood. 'Oh, sweetheart!'

He was sobbing. 'I told them to back away. I told them to stay quiet and back away, but they wouldn't listen.'

Oh, lord, he was talking! He was *talking*!

'Sam, are you OK? Sam! Sam!' Josh, the younger brother, was sobbing, too.

Luke had dropped to the ground beside the boy. 'The

bird's gone, Sam, it's OK,' he said, sounding clear and calm and strong. If anyone could give an injured child confidence, it would be Luke. 'It's over now.' He threw another couple of words over his shoulder to Janey. 'He's hurt.'

Badly, she knew from his tone. She already knew it from the bleeding, although neither of them had wanted to say it in front of the three kids. And they had no equipment with them.

'Femoral artery,' Luke finished.

Arriving beside him, she saw that he'd already rolled Sam into a better position and thrust his hand against the wound to stop the bleeding, which would prove fatal within minutes if it wasn't checked. There were already frightening amounts of blood on the ground, soaking Sam's clothing and splotched on Josh as well. Sam's shorts and T-shirt were both badly torn.

'I'll check airway and breathing.' She knew Luke would have to keep his hand where it was for at least ten minutes, and that his muscles would be screaming and stiff from the awkward action by the end of it. She could see the uncomfortable posture he'd had to take up.

They couldn't even think of moving Sam or going for help yet. 'Sam, Josh, I'm a doctor,' she told the boys, 'and so is Luke here, so you're going to be OK. We know exactly what to do so, Sam, sweetheart, try and answer my questions. Can you do that?'

He must have been terrified. Must still be terrified at the sight of so much of his own blood staining the dirt, ebbing away. They had to keep him calm and reassured if they possibly could, and Rowdy and Josh, too. The two younger boys had moved to sit slump-shouldered in the shade of a bush at the side of the path, silently watching.

And Rowdy had spoken.

Luke looked in his son's direction and swore harshly under his breath, before muttering to Janey, 'I want so damn much to find out—' He stopped.

'I know. But we can't. This is more urgent.'

'I know that. Hell, I do, but…'

Their eyes met, reflecting shared anguish and frustration, and she felt the same intense relief and rightness as she'd felt last night beside the pool at the fact that the two of them were there together, that this was Luke, not anyone else in the world. The past didn't matter any more. The fact that he'd been Alice's husband. The fact that he didn't remember their long-ago kiss. The fact that they'd spent half the night in each other's arms. There was only now.

'Sam, first, are you having any trouble breathing?' she asked the boy. 'Show me a nice deep breath.'

He drew one in, but stopped before he'd filled his lungs, and said thinly, 'It hurts.'

She caught Luke's glance again, and knew he'd be running through the same possibilities that she was. If one of those shockingly forceful thrusts had broken some ribs which had punctured his lungs… How would they cope with pneumothorax and respiratory arrest here?

Janey laid her hands on his chest, and said, 'Keep breathing, Sam, just normally.'

'You're doing great,' Luke came in. 'I've stopped the bleeding in your leg now, but I'll have to keep my hand here for a while longer, OK?'

'OK…'

'Boys, we need to do a bit of work on him before we get him back to the resort and ready for airlifting to hospital, so you must help by sitting patiently. Rowdy,

have some of your water, and see if Josh wants some.'
Rowdy nodded and began unzipping the day pack.

'Josh, are you guys with your parents? Are you
staying on the island?'

'They're in our cabin,' Josh said. 'Having a rest.'

'OK, we'll talk to them as soon as we can, but for
now stay with us, all right?'

'All right.'

'Can't feel anything broken,' Janey told Luke.

'Rising equally on both sides?'

'From what I can feel.' Which was good, as far as it
went, but she would have liked a greater degree of cer-
tainty. 'If we had a stethoscope…'

'We can't move him yet. Where does it hurt, Sam?'

'Everywhere. My leg, my stomach…' His voice was
shaky but clear, which meant his airway was clear, too.
That was a plus.

'I'm going to take a look at you now,' Janey said. 'I'm
going to lift up your shirt. How about you close your
eyes and just rest?'

She had to clamp her mouth shut over a hiss of breath
when she saw the claw marks across Sam's body. There
was a big, red, bruising welt at the top left of his
abdomen, just nudging his lower ribs, and then a gash
raking down and getting deeper until its final disastrous
hook into the top of the thigh.

A couple of shallower gashes crossed the deeper one
at a slight angle, and there was another nasty wound
lower on his thigh, from which blood still trickled
slowly. She palpated his abdomen and he whimpered
and moved his hands defensively when she got to that
upper left quadrant, beneath the blotchy welt.

'That's where it hurts most?'

'Yes. Badly.'

Luke looked at her again, and they were both thinking about injury to the spleen. Sam was white as a ghost, almost green. She took his pulse at the neck, and found the rapid rhythm she'd expected—about 120 beats a minute.

'Can you find a radial pulse?' Luke muttered.

She moved her fingers to Sam's wrist, and reported after several seconds, 'Yes, just. It's faint.'

'We need to get him to the medical centre. They have one. I saw a blue and white cross on that map.'

Kids were different to adults. They compensated well for blood loss initially, and then crashed catastrophically later on, if you didn't get in fast with oxygen and fluids.

'We need to make a pressure bandage,' she answered, not a retort but a recognition there was more to be done before they could move him. She pulled her T-shirt over her head, thankful that she still had Georgie's swimsuit on beneath it. She began to fold the fabric into a pad.

Luke flicked his gaze away from the sight of the valley between her breasts, and she felt the heat of their shared awareness and emotion once more, before it fled in the face of the urgency of what they had to do. He asked Sam, 'Can you wiggle your fingers and toes? Any pins and needles?' Could that gash to the thigh have gone deep enough to compromise movement and nerves?

Sam's answers were the ones they wanted to hear, but his voice sounded much weaker.

'I can't move my hand away yet,' Luke said. 'Can you rip up my shirt while I'm wearing it, Janey, without moving us around too much?'

'I'll try.'

'Use your teeth, if you need to.'

She did need to. The woven cotton fabric was new and strongly stitched. Kneeling beside him, she lifted the lower edge of the shirt away from his body and bent to grit her teeth against it, near the side seam, aware of his hot, tanned skin just inches away.

She smelt sunscreen and salt, and saw the stretch and knot of his muscles. In any other situation she would have wanted to press her lips to his body and taste him, run her fingers all over him, the way she had last night. She couldn't remember ever wanting a man this much before—this simply, this physically. It felt as natural as breathing, as solid as gravity, some kind of chemical shift in her that related in a weird way to all the old irritation.

Maybe it hadn't been pure irritation, eight years ago, at all...

They'd kissed on Wednesday night, they'd made love in Luke's dark bedroom with Rowdy just down the corridor, and now they were working together like two pieces of well-oiled machinery, and all of it just felt so inevitable she didn't even have a name for it.

The fabric ripped up the side as she pulled, then she had to use her teeth again to get it to rip parallel to the hem, her knuckles and cheeks bumping against his smooth, strong back several times as she worked. 'Sorry about this, Luke.'

'It's fine.' Gritted teeth. His arm must be knotting from the unrelenting pressure he had to keep against Sam's thigh.

Janey ended up with three bands of fabric, each about ten centimetres wide, while Luke wore half a shirt. 'That's great,' he said. 'Let's do this now.'

They pressed her folded shirt into the wound and bound it tightly with the strips of Luke's shirt. He pulled the remnant of the garment from his body, his muscles and smooth tan on show, and deftly ripped some final pieces to fasten the pressure bandage more securely.

Sam was way too quiet. Whimpering faintly. Eyes closed. Sweaty and still that deathly greenish-white. He'd lost a lot of blood before Luke had been able to act to stop it and he could be bleeding internally. They needed to get oxygen and fluid replacement in place urgently now, because despite the reassurances they'd given him—and had been right to give, because the worst thing you could do was let someone know how serious their injuries were—if he went into irreversible shock, he would die.

'I'm going to carry him back along the trail,' Luke said. 'It'll buy us a few minutes' more time. Janey, go on ahead as fast as you can. We saw that helipad. He'll need an airlift down south. And I saw a couple of those electric buggy things that the resort staff use. Try and—'

'I know. I'll find someone. I'll bring transport.' She didn't mess around, just rose and began to sprint back down the trail.

Rowdy scrambled to his feet, too. 'Wait, Auntie Janey…' He followed her, and if he wanted to come with her, she wasn't going to leave him behind. Oh, lord, he was speaking at last, and they'd had no time to talk about it or think about it or even give him a decent hug!

She grabbed his hand and pulled him along, hearing Luke say to Josh behind her, 'Come on, mate, we'll be a bit slower.'

Thank goodness Rowdy was a little wild bush kid! Despite his small size and all he had been through recently, he was fit and strong and could keep up. They were both panting by the time the first of the resort buildings came into view, and her lungs burned.

One of the resort buggies went trundling round the back of the aviary and she chased after it and yelled at the uniformed staff person at the wheel. 'We have a seriously wounded child back on the trail. We need help!'

The buggy slowed, stopped, reversed, turned, came trundling back. She explained, fighting her breathlessness. 'He got attacked by a cassowary—'

'Hell! Elke!'

'What?'

'It must have been Elke.' The man swore again. 'Get in.'

He reached out to pull on Rowdy's arm, and helped them both into the storage well behind the vehicle's one pair of seats. The passenger seat was crowded with gear. Janey sat Rowdy on her lap, because there was nothing to keep him from falling out through the buggy's low, open sides.

They shot back down the trail while the man explained, 'There are no cassowaries in the wild on Charm Island. But we had a pair in the animal park, hoping to get them to breed in June or July. Half the aviary went in the cyclone. We lost almost all the birds, escaped or killed. We found Fred, the male cassowary, but we couldn't find Elke. We were starting to think she hadn't survived.'

'Well, she did, and she's up in the rainforest, and she's hurt and she's incredibly dangerous,' Janey told him. 'The boy has some serious injuries, femoral artery bleeding, and he's going into shock.'

The man swore again. 'Where's the bird now?'

'Disappeared back into the forest. Scared off, or in pain.'

'We have to find her, or she'll hurt someone else. But they're so damned hard to find and catch!'

'I want to think about this casualty first. Do you have a two-way radio? He'll need the air medical service, and I really hope you have a well-equipped medical centre at the resort! Is your helipad back in action?'

'Yes. I'll call it in right now.' He seemed organised and on the ball. Steering with one hand, he put the walkie-talkie to his ear, pressed a button and spoke. 'We have a code six on the mountain trail, John. Repeating, that's a code six.'

Seconds later, Janey heard a crackling response but couldn't make out the words.

'There,' the man said.

'That's enough?'

'Code six. Require emergency medical evacuation by air off the island.' He looked a little shaky and green suddenly. 'I've never had to call one in for a kid before. And it's lucky we've got the medical centre. We used to send people over to Wallaby Island in our motor launch for anything more than a cut finger, but their centre got demolished by Cyclone Willie. My name's Andrew, by the way.'

'I'm glad you have your systems in place, Andrew.' She gave Rowdy a reassuring squeeze on her lap, desperately wishing she could take some time out to talk to him about what had happened. Not yet. They couldn't do it yet. And she needed Luke.

'We should reach them soon, right?' Andrew asked.

They both saw Luke and the two boys at that moment, ahead on the trail. Luke's strides were still long and smooth as he tried not to jolt his fragile cargo, but he'd begun to stagger beneath the boy's weight. Sam must weigh twice what Rowdy did. The muscles in Luke's calves and upper arms had knotted tight. The pressure bandage must be holding, thank goodness, or he would have stopped.

Andrew pulled the vehicle to a halt and unceremoniously dumped the equipment from the passenger seat onto the trail—tools and a tarpaulin, from what Janey could see. 'Stay in the back, guys,' he told her and Rowdy. 'Mate, you'll have to squeeze in, too,' he said to Josh, who was gasping, breathless and tearful. It was crowded, but they managed. Janey put one arm around the shaken younger boy.

Luke climbed in, cradling the injured Sam in his arms. 'Can't feel a radial pulse any more,' he said tersely to Janey. And added then to Andrew, 'What medical facilities do you have here?'

'There's a medical centre with a nurse, pretty new. I'm sorry, I can't tell you exactly what they have and don't have on hand.'

'We'll manage. It'll be half an hour before the chopper can get here.' Maybe longer, Janey knew. Again, Luke didn't want to talk about worst-case scenarios out loud. If the chopper was already out on another call... 'Sam, you're going to be fine, OK? You've got two doctors taking care of you, and more on the way. Josh, you said your mum and dad are at your cabin?'

Andrew cut in, 'What number is it, mate, do you know?'

'Twenty-two,' Josh said.

Andrew got back on his radio, his other hand swinging the steering-wheel smoothly. They were almost back at the resort. 'Code nine to cabin twenty-two, and bring them straight to the medical centre.'

'Code nine,' Luke echoed.

'Notifying relatives of an illness or injury.'

'Who thought this up?'

'The boss. Used to be a mess, crackling radios and messages getting mucked up all over the shop. Want to guess what code one is, the one we need most often?' he drawled.

'Send a cleaner with a mop,' Janey came in promptly.

'You got it.' The moment of humour came as a short-lived relief to the tension.

'You're doing great, Sam,' Luke said. 'Just keep breathing for me. Just relax, and don't move. You're going to be fine.'

They reached the main building, the buggy scooting to within inches of the entrance, and Janey saw what had to be the medical centre through a door to the left. They left Josh and Rowdy in Andrew's care. 'Ice creams?' he mouthed at Janey, and she nodded, before hurrying inside behind Luke and Sam.

There was a nurse in attendance, comfortably built, in her forties, unflappable, and she didn't need to be told how serious Sam's injuries were. She took one look at him and began pulling equipment into place at once.

'I'm Dr Bresciano from Crocodile Creek Hospital,' Luke said. 'And this is Dr Stafford, who's in general practice in Darwin. Luke and Janey.'

'Right.' The nurse nodded. 'That's lucky for all of us.' She added casually, 'You must know Dr Wetherby.'

'Charles. He's great. It's hard to reconcile what he achieves with the fact that he's in a wheelchair.'

The nurse nodded, and Janey knew that Luke had passed her subtle check of his credentials by his use of the medical director's first name and knowledge of his circumstances. They got Sam onto the examining table and set up an oxygen supply, using a non-rebreather mask at fifteen litres a minute.

Janey used a stethoscope to give his breathing a more thorough check than she'd been able to out on the hiking trail, and couldn't find any evidence of broken ribs, a punctured lung or other respiratory problems. But his heart rate and breathing were still far too fast, and his oxygen saturation had dropped to 94 per cent. They didn't have much time.

The nurse—'Barb,' she'd told them in a quick aside— attempted to take a blood-pressure reading, but shrugged and shook her head. The pressure had dropped too low, which meant a dangerous level of blood loss and shock.

Sam needed urgent IV access, but it was a catch-22 situation. His circulation had shut down too far for them to find a vein. Luke tightened a tourniquet around the boy's arm, but there was still nothing. 'Janey, what do you think?' he asked in a fast undertone. 'Cut-down or central vein?'

'Central vein. He needs this done fast, Luke.'

'I think so, too.' Their shoulders bumped together. 'Unless you're really smooth on cut-downs?'

'No, not that smooth.'

'We'll go with the right jugular.' The large vein would take the rapid infusion of fluid that Sam now urgently needed. 'Sam, we're going to put in a drip needle to give you some fluid, OK? You'll feel a bit of a sting, because I'm going to give you some painkiller through the needle first, but then it won't hurt and it'll be taped in place and it will make you feel a lot stronger and better. Barb, is there a microwave?'

'You want to warm the fluids?'

'Yes, please, if we can.'

Janey adjusted Sam's position gently, turning his head away so that he wouldn't see Luke's approach with the needle and tilting his head down slightly to distend the vein. Luke prepared the drugs and found the carotid pulse on the neck. The internal jugular would run parallel a short distance to the side. Janey couldn't help watching the long, lean shapes of his fingers as he worked. Surgeons performed miracles with their hands, the way dancers performed miracles with their bodies.

He injected the painkiller then, with the fingers of his left hand still marking the position of the artery, slipped the needle in half a centimetre away at an angle of forty-five degrees and kept up a gentle pressure.

Janey saw the moment when he entered the vein, at about three centimetres' depth. Blood came into the syringe, and he used his thumb over the hub of the needle to stop any air going in. He inserted the guide wire, removed the needle, loaded the cannula and pushed it into the vein, his movements fast and sure.

Janey grabbed a blood-pressure cuff and when Luke had aspirated some blood from the vein to check its placement and connected the cannula to the infusion equipment, she put the cuff onto the bag of fluid and pumped it up tight to squeeze the fluid through the tubing and into Sam's body as fast as possible.

'OK, that's great,' Luke said. 'That's brilliant. Sam, you're doing fine, and that's the hard part over.'

They hoped.

'Need another cuff?' said Barb.

'Yes, let's see if we've got some pressure now.' They all held their breath. Eighty over forty. It had come up, but was still too low.

'He's getting seepage,' Janey said. The new, spreading stain looked rusty pink against the pale blue, grey and cream pattern of Luke's torn shirt fabric.

'I don't want to disturb the dressing. It's too pretty,' Luke said, for Sam's benefit.

'Second dressing on top?' Barb asked.

'Think so, at this point.'

They heard voices outside, angry and upset and scared. Sam's parents, and Josh. 'I'll go and talk to them,' Janey said, while Luke and Barb began to put the second dressing in place.

In the foyer outside the medical centre she found Sam's mother sobbing and his father white-lipped, helpless and angry, with Andrew and Rowdy and Josh there, too. The boys had finished their ice creams and had sticky mouths.

'They're saying it was a bird,' the father yelled. 'How could a bloody bird have ripped open his whole leg? Why aren't there any bloody warning signs? How can you have vicious, dangerous wildlife roaming around a family holiday resort, for heck's sake? Are you people insane?'

'We're going to find the bird, Mr Marshall,' Andrew said, trying to placate him.

'Is he going to be all right?' the mother sobbed. 'Can I see him? Just tell me he's all right.'

'And shoot it on the bloody spot. And any others on the island.'

'He's doing well, Mrs Marshall,' Janey said. 'You'll be able to see him very soon, once we have him sorted out with fluids and medication.'

Luke appeared and was quickly introduced. 'We're getting him stable—he did lose a fair bit of blood,' he said. He stood tall, his height giving a natural air of confidence and authority. The kind of man any parent would trust. Eight years ago he'd come across as cocky and arrogant and far too sure of himself. Now he was a man you'd lean on to the ends of the earth, and you'd feel safe all the way.

'We have fluid going in, and he's on oxygen,' he continued. 'There may be an internal injury to the spleen, although signs are that it wouldn't be major. That'll be checked out more thoroughly when he gets to hospital. We have a chopper on its way, and one of you will be able to go in it with him, Mrs Marshall. I'll take you in to see him in a moment.'

'Yeah, and what about the next kid playing on the nature trail? The bird has to be shot!'

But Janey had felt Rowdy stiffen beside her. 'Don't shoot her,' he said, almost in a whisper. His little hand came creeping into hers and his cheek pressed against her lower arm. 'She was hurt and scared. The boys wouldn't back away. She couldn't help it. Cassowaries are endangered.'

He looked crumpled and weary and defeated, immune to the healing powers of ice cream. She caught Luke's agonised glance.

'Let me handle things here for a bit,' he said, stepping to within inches of her and lowering his head so that they couldn't be overheard. She felt his body warmth and the effort of his iron control. Just wanted to rest against the rock-like strength of his body but knew she couldn't. Not now. 'I've got Barb. You have to talk to him, Janey.' His voice shook. 'I can't bear to leave him in the lurch like this! For five years I didn't know where he was, and now he needs me and I can't be there. If it wasn't for you, I don't know what I'd do.'

'Luke—'

'Just go.'

She nodded at him, took Rowdy's hand and walked him outside, to where they could see a stretch of beach and the boat jetty and various holidaymakers enjoying their afternoon.

'I don't want them to shoot her,' Rowdy said again. 'I want them to find her and make her hurt leg better.'

'I know you do.'

Oh, lord, what should she say? Should she make a promise about Elke's safety that might be impossible to keep? Or prepare Rowdy for the worst? Sometimes rogue wildlife had to be killed.

'I don't know if that's going to be possible, love,' she said in the end. 'Maybe she hurt herself too badly in the cyclone. Sometimes when an animal's been hurt it's just not ever going to be well enough to take care of itself in the wild.'

'Elke's not wild. She can go back in the bird place.'

'She might be too aggressive to catch safely. We'll talk to Andrew about it in a minute. He seems good, doesn't he?'

'Yes. We could show him where she went into the bush, and follow her tracks, and they could get a vet and give her medicine and bandage her up like you bandaged Sam.'

'Hey...let's not think about Elke for the moment. You're talking again!'

'I had to, to warn those boys, but they wouldn't listen. I didn't want to. I wouldn't have talked if I didn't have to.' Did he think she would be angry?

'It's fine, love. It's fine. And it wasn't so bad, was it? The talking? It felt OK, didn't it? Nothing terrible—'

But Rowdy wasn't listening to this.

'Where's Mum, Auntie Janey?' he cut in, as if he couldn't wait another second to say it. His little voice trembled, and the trust and silent pleading in his eyes made them as big as saucers. 'They took her away to a wonderful place, Raina said. To get better. Isn't she going to be better and coming back soon? Nobody's told me. I stayed quiet, quiet, quiet for as long as I could to help her heal. Isn't it working yet?'

CHAPTER EIGHT

LUKE took Jason and Simone Marshall into the medical centre, stopping them just inside the door to say quietly, 'He'll need your reassurance.'

Not your anger or your tears, please, for his sake, no matter how emotional you are feeling.

How much should he spell it out? Mr Marshall still looked explosive, while his wife made no effort to hold back her sobs. Luke himself was struggling internally. He felt as if half his soul had gone with Janey and his son, only he couldn't follow, and couldn't let his emotion show. In microcosm, it was what he'd endured for five years while Rowdy had been lost to him, and the only thing that made it bearable was Janey.

Not Alice. Janey.

He lowered his voice a little further, and told the Marshalls, 'He's had a big shock and your attitude is very important at this point. We can talk later about whether the resort is to blame, and what that means in terms of action. For now, he needs to see you smiling.'

'Yes, Jase, please?' Simone laid a hand on her husband's arm and gathered her own control with a huge effort. She had peeling, sunburned skin, making the lines of strain around her mouth crease tighter.

Jason nodded and said gruffly, 'As long as he's OK. That's all that matters.'

Luke moved forward. 'Sam, your mum and dad are here.'

'We're here now, mate. It's OK. It's OK.'

'Love, oh, love.' Simone kissed her son and stroked his forehead.

Barb took Luke aside. 'I'm afraid there's more seepage coming through the dressing.'

'Take another BP.'

Seventy over forty, they found. It had dropped again.

'We're going to have to tie off the artery,' Luke decided out loud. 'He can't afford to lose any more blood, and we can't ship him out in this condition. Have you got what we need? Artery forceps? Clamps?'

Barb nodded. 'I'll have everything ready for you.'

'I'll talk to the parents, get them to go back out. I would have liked to give them more time with him, but…'

'But we need to do this, if we're going to. And not in front of them.'

'Yes.' He had to deal with Jason and Simone Marshall's stricken faces when he told them their son needed more urgent intervention, and they'd have to wait outside.

Next, he washed and gloved up, knowing he'd need to move fast as soon as the artery was exposed. Once Barb had removed the old dressing and applied manual pressure, he swabbed the wound and found the end of the artery before blood filled the area and obscured it from view. He clamped it and that scary welling of blood stopped. Another swab cleared the area and he tied off the artery.

Sam would need a good vascular surgeon in Brisbane, and possibly a laparotomy if they discovered bleeding from the spleen, but for now they'd done all they could. He re-dressed the wound and told Barb, 'Bring them back in. They should be able to stay with him now until the chopper gets here.'

A few minutes later Barb was able to report, 'Blood pressure up to eighty-five over forty-two now. Oxygen sat at ninety-seven.'

The sound of chopper blades cutting the air began to thrum in their ears.

Janey sat beside Rowdy on the sand.

Her jaw and eyes and throat ached and stung from tension and unshed tears. She couldn't let herself cry, because her precious nephew—this sturdy, stricken little being—didn't need tears from her right now. He needed the best words in the world, and she wasn't sure that those words even existed. 'But it just wasn't enough,' she said, 'and the ambulance came too late, and so she died.'

'She died in the ambulance.'

'Yes, sweetheart.'

'I knew she died.' He sounded so bleak and defeated, confronted with the stark reality that his magical thinking had failed.

Magical thinking.

Should they have guessed, she and Luke? Should they have understood and known? He was only five. Death was such an abstract, impossible concept for him, even though he must have seen it in the bush many times—lizards and birds.

I knew she died.

He'd known it and not known it, both at the same

time. Kids could do that, and even adults could some-times. He had pinned himself heroically to those mixed-up concepts in his little mind and to the hope in his warm little heart. That if he stayed quiet, his mum would get better. That she'd gone to a wonderful place to get better, and somehow his desperate silence would move the necessary mountains and bring her back.

But if he spoke, the spell would be broken.

If he spoke, he'd have to ask the questions he desperately wanted to ask and hear the answers which he was so desperately afraid of.

Because really, in his heart, he'd known…

She held him, hoping that her touch might be enough, even though words just weren't, wishing with all her heart that Luke was there. 'But I'm your Auntie Janey, Rowdy,' she whispered. 'I'm your mum's sister, and I love you, and I even look a little bit like her…'

'You look quite a lot like her.'

'Do I?'

'Yes.'

'Well, I know it's not the same as having Mum, but I will take care of you and we'll go to Melbourne soon for a holiday, and you can see your grandma and grandpa, because they love you, too.'

'Who are they, my grandma and grandpa?'

Why didn't you ever talk about us, Alice? Why did you always want to burn your boats and reject your own past?

'They're my mum and dad, and your mum's mum and dad,' she said.

'I didn't know I had them. And who's Luke? Is he my uncle?' He sounded cautious about it, just a little bit hopeful, she thought.

'He's—he's a good friend. He's someone who cares

about you, too, very much.' Because she didn't think she could tell him the truth just yet, not without Luke himself there. It had to be his decision, not hers.

'Are we going to live at Mundarri?' Rowdy asked.

'No, not there. Because I'm a doctor and I need to work in a town or a city, where there are more people to be my patients.'

'So where?'

'Somewhere good.' She couldn't tell him blankly that she didn't know, couldn't leave him on shifting ground when everything in his whole world had shifted so much already. She added, 'We'll think about it, and decide together. But I promise you, it'll be somewhere good.'

The sound of chopper rotors in the distance came to their ears and grew rapidly louder. It had come for Sam, and she knew she should get back to the medical centre to see if she was needed to help with the transfer.

She told Rowdy, 'You did a great job, trying to warn those kids about the cassowary. It wasn't your fault that they didn't listen. I think they were too scared.'

'It wasn't her fault either. She was hurt and she was scared, too. She didn't know how bad it is to hurt a kid like that. She thought they were going to hurt her.'

'I know, love.'

'I want her to be healed. I don't want her to die. She needs to mate with Fred and lay eggs. He'll sit on them for her and they'll hatch.'

'You know all about it, don't you? Is it the male that sits on the eggs?'

'With cassowaries it is.'

'We'd better get back and see how Sam is doing.'

'When can we see how Elke is doing?' He stood up

and took her hand again, and the simple little gesture of trust almost broke her heart.

I cannot let this child down. Ever.

'We'll ask Andrew,' she said. 'He'll know what we can do.'

'I want her to be healed,' he repeated, and Janey wondered about the issue's importance in his mind, if it was connected with Alice somehow—his own mother, and the female bird—and how much his trust in happy endings might be permanently damaged if the adults around him shrugged at Elke's plight or went out and shot her in cold blood.

She saw the helicopter touch down, its rotors blasting the surrounding vegetation in a mimicry of the cyclone's recent destruction. Two flight paramedics emerged with a wheeled stretcher, and there was trusty Andrew, guiding them to the medical centre. She followed, but found that everything was under control, with Sam being shifted to the stretcher, covered in a light blanket, and with fluid and oxygen still going in.

Luke reported, 'We had to tie off the artery and re-dress the wound. He's looking more stable now, blood pressure's up, respiration's slowed, but there may be a way still to go.'

'Spleen damage?'

'Won't be surprised. Not huge, but something's going on in there, I think. The leg'll need some attention, and those other wounds. We gave them a swab and started antibiotics, but that was all we had time for. The mum's flying with him, and the dad and Josh will pack up here, catch the boat over to the mainland and start the drive down tonight.' He dropped his voice further. 'How is he? Still talking?'

She didn't need to ask who he meant by 'he.'

'Oh, Luke, wait till you hear what's been going on in his head…' Her voice cracked. 'But what's urgent for him now is Elke, the bird. I want to ask Andrew if there's a wildlife officer or a park ranger. If there's any chance that she doesn't have to be killed, and that a vet can work on that wound…'

They went with the paramedics to the chopper, trundling along one of the wooden boardwalks that led between various parts or the resort, while Simone and Jason Marshall made confused plans. Which hospital were they going to? Where would he stop for the night along the way? What time did the boat run? Who did they need to phone?

One of the paramedics—Luke knew him, apparently, he was based in Crocodile Creek, Rhys someone—said to them, 'Looks like it was touch and go. Bloody lucky you two were here.'

'Don't even say it!'

'Where's the bird?'

'That's the next question now that Sam is stable,' Luke answered. 'Although as far as you guys go, I wouldn't rest on your laurels during the ride.' He told Rhys about the suspected spleen injury and the gashes they hadn't had time to examine closely or treat.

'Fill you in next time I see you,' Rhys said.

They loaded Sam aboard with impressive speed and efficiency while Janey, Luke, Rowdy, Andrew, Josh and Jason stood on the boardwalk at a safe distance and watched. Janey took advantage of the lull and told Luke about what Rowdy had said.

'That's why? Oh, lord…'

The doors closed and the rotors whirred into life

again, ready to lift Sam off into the blue promise of clear skies for flying and a major hospital down south.

A young woman appeared along the wide wooden boardwalk seconds after the helicopter had taken off, professionally smiling and perky, summoned by one of Andrew's radio codes. Hospitality staff? He told her, 'Help Mr Marshall and his son with everything they need to do to pack and check out and get the boat, would you, Lauren?'

She nodded and introduced herself to Jason and Josh, then led them in the direction of their cabin, making shocked and soothing sounds when she heard their story.

As soon as Lauren and the Marshalls had gone, Luke said quietly to Andrew, 'Something needs to be done about the bird, and we're hoping that doesn't just mean a hunt and a bullet.'

'I've been trying to contact Ben Chandler, the head ranger on Wallaby Island, to get his advice. There are only three rangers in North Queensland qualified to handle injured cassowaries, and fortunately he's one of them. This is beyond the realm of our aviary staff. He's supposed to be calling me back. Most of the island's shut down over there because of cyclone damage, but I know he's around, and he's good.'

'Working around the clock, I imagine.'

'Aren't we all? I'm sure he won't want the bird killed if we can possibly avoid it, because they're a protected species and numbers have dropped dangerously low in the wild. Let me get back to my office and see if we've heard from him yet. It's around the corner of the building from the medical centre, if you want to check back in a little while. Or you can phone from the mainland later on and I'll give you an update.'

'Thanks, Andrew.' After he'd gone, Luke turned to Janey. 'Should we head back? That five o'clock boat we planned on taking is leaving soon.' The dazzling heat and colour had just begun to fade, and the air felt cooler. There was a fresh breeze blowing. It would be lovely out on the water.

She nodded. 'I guess that makes sense.'

But when they told Rowdy about the plan his little face went tight and pale, even though he only nodded. Janey couldn't stand to see the defeat and resignation in his face. She bent to his level. 'You don't want to go back yet, do you? You want to wait and see if Elke is safe first.'

He burst into tears. 'She can't die. I don't want her to die.'

'Oh, sweetheart…' Suddenly Janey was crying too, aching for him.

'Mum died…'

'I know, and we're all sad about it, and there hasn't been—' Her voice caught '—time to cry.'

'I didn't say goodbye to her.'

To that, there were no words.

The two of them hugged hard, and then Luke was there, too, crouching down with his arms hard and warm around both of them, his strong shoulders shuddering and his lips pressed tight together. Rowdy cried and cried and cried, and neither Janey nor Luke tried to stop him or tried to say anything of comfort, because the best thing seemed to be just this.

Holding each other.

Letting the tears come, for as along as they wanted.

If they earned a few curious or concerned glances from people passing by, they didn't care.

When it was finally over, they all felt a little better. Rowdy said, 'We can help them with Elke. I want to.'

'What do you think we could do, sweetheart?' Janey asked.

'We could show them the place where she ran into the rainforest. We could follow her tracks.'

'Let me talk about it with Luke.' She straightened and stood, not knowing what to do, needing Luke's input. 'Want to have another look in the gift shop while we do that?' she asked Rowdy.

'OK.'

They walked back to the sprawl of the main resort building and let him wander in the gift shop on his own, keeping an eye on him from where they stood on the deck just outside the gift-shop door.

'It's important to him,' Luke said. 'Pretty obvious why.'

'Because he needs a happy ending. But if it ends badly, if they can't find her or if they do have to destroy her, will it make things worse?'

'Except maybe it's not a happy ending he needs,' he said slowly. 'Maybe it's just an ending, a clean, un-equivocal one, the kind he never got with Alice.'

'Even if it's a bad ending?' She searched his face. 'If they decide to put Elke down? Are we prepared to take that risk?'

'I don't see that we have a choice. He'll want to know the truth, whether he's there to witness it or not. And I don't think we should try to hide the truth from him.'

'No, you're right, we can't do that.'

'If those women at Mundarri—I know they meant well but if they'd been clearer to him about the truth of Alice's death, he would have had an easier time. He would have been able to ask questions instead of believing he had to bottle them all up. Janey, I think we have to stay on here until we have an answer for him.'

She nodded, and he took her hands and squeezed them, then bent his head to rest on her shoulder for a moment. His cheek brushed against hers, but he didn't kiss her. Neither of them spoke. She didn't know what the moment meant but valued it anyway just because, as always, connecting with him seemed to keep her feet on solid ground.

They collected Rowdy from the gift shop and headed for the resort office to find Andrew. He met them halfway, striding at a rapid pace, with his walkie-talkie pressed to his ear. When he saw them, he said, 'There's been another sighting, and Ben is already on his way by boat from Wallaby Island. He has a vet with him. She's been helping him with the injured wildlife, and she's had experience with cassowaries, too.'

'Where was Elke seen?'

'There's a bird-watching hide at the end of a walking loop that runs off the rainforest trail. Ben thinks she might be drawn to human contact because she was raised in captivity. She associates people with food. A couple of serious parrot botherers spotted her through their binoculars and saw that she was hurt.'

'Parrot botherers?'

'Amateur birdwatchers. But she disappeared into the rainforest again. Ben reckons it'll be bloody hard to catch her if she doesn't want to be found. We've closed all three trails now. We gave each of them a sweep by vehicle and got people to cut short their hikes and head back, but the birdwatchers had gone off the trail in search of a cross-eyed, red-belted fig-whistler—'

'That's not a real bird name!' Rowdy whispered to Janey indignantly.

'And we missed them. Let me show you on the map, and you can tell me how the location relates to where you saw her. Ben should be here very soon, and I'd like to have something concrete to tell him about where to start looking.'

He led the way to the big, colourful map board that showed the whole resort, complete with stylised palm trees, pictures of cabins and boat-launching places, and even a mermaid splashing her tail in the water.

'This can't be drawn to scale,' Luke said.

'No, it isn't. I hate these things. I like real maps, with a scale and contour lines and grid references. But those don't make the resort look so pretty and interesting.' He pointed on the map to something that looked like a grass hut. 'Here's the bird-watching hide. It has windows covering an outlook of 270 degrees, and the birdwatchers reckon they were looking in this direction.' He made an angled line with his hand.

'That's back towards where we must have been on the mountain trail when Elke attacked Sam.'

'Show me the spot.'

'Here.' Luke pointed. 'Janey, Rowdy, do you reckon?'

'We crossed a bridge over a little creek, with rocks,' Rowdy said.

'You're right, we did, I'd forgotten. So if that's accurate—' he pointed to the stylised picture of a bridge, surrounded by tree ferns '—then we were a bit further than I said. About here.'

Andrew circled his finger over the map. 'And this is pretty thick rainforest, all through here, between the trail and the hide. So maybe she's taken up residence somewhere in there.'

'She might like the creek,' Rowdy said.

'She might. And Ben could use it for access, because it runs right through the centre of the rainforest and the vegetation gets dense in there.'

'That's great, Rowdy.'

'Can we come, too?' he asked.

Janey and Luke exchanged looks. She pressed her lips together and gave an imperceptible shake of her head. Her memory of the cassowary kicking Sam so viciously with that razor-sharp claw, more than six inches long, was too fresh and real. She didn't want to go back on that trail with a child, even with other adults around. Those little buggies didn't offer much protection.

'I think he needs to do this, Janey,' Luke said quietly.

She shook her head harder. 'No.'

'And he might be of real help. He's observant, and he knows his birds.'

'No, Luke, I—'

He turned to Andrew. 'How about if we take a ride to the bird hide in one of those buggies and watch from there? And if you had a spare walkie-talkie for us? She might get flushed back to that spot if she's disturbed in the thicker forest.' He dropped his voice. 'Janey? Good compromise? We'll all be safe in the hide, but he'll be genuinely involved, too.'

This time she nodded. 'Thanks. I was overreacting, I guess.'

'Believe me, I knew what you were thinking.'

'We'd appreciate the help,' Andrew said. 'I don't want to create a panic through the whole resort by turning this into a major search, but we have to find her. If we don't by morning then we'll have to close the place down. Even with the trails off limits, the risk is too great now that we know that she can and will seek out human contact and then attack so viciously.'

'You have somewhere to put her?'

'Fred's doing fine in his temporary cage. We have a crew starting tomorrow, getting the aviary back in operation.' He looked out at the water, where an official-looking motor launch was speeding towards the dock. 'That's Ben and the vet. Let's get this sorted.'

It was quiet and still in the hide, and even now that it had been thinned in places by Cyclone Willie, the thickness of the surrounding vegetation meant that any sounds from the water or the resort could barely be heard. The hide smelt of new, treated wood and varnish.

Rowdy stood on one of the raised benches that allowed small children to see through the unglassed windows that overlooked the rainforest clearing. Janey sat beside him, her body twisted so she could rest one elbow on the wooden sill. Littered on the ground was a pile of rainforest fruit. It had been placed there and in a couple of other spots where they'd have a good chance at capturing the wounded bird if the fruit lured her.

'I can't see anything,' Rowdy said.

The walkie-talkie in Luke's hand crackled with voices occasionally. He couldn't make out all of the exchanges. None of them were addressed to him.

'Off the side of the trail, Ben,' he heard.

'At the creek? Over!'

'Hearing something in the undergrowth, but they move so damned quietly.'

'Tell us your position now, over.'

One voice belonged to the vet, Julie Nguyen, and

another to wildlife officer Ben Chandler. Luke also heard Andrew and another resort staffer.

'Where is she?' Rowdy said.

'Might have to be pretty patient, love,' Janey told him.

She watched Rowdy more than she watched for the cassowary.

And Luke watched her.

She had sand and salt stuck to her legs and a mist of sweat on her back. The strap of Georgie's scarlet swimsuit was twisted on one shoulder, and her denim shorts had dirt marks in several places. Her sandals were covered in dried mud. She looked hot and tired, but she didn't complain or pace around, just sat and watched Rowdy, or occasionally the clearing, and waited for the clean-cut ending they were all hoping for.

So different from Alice, and yet they did look alike sometimes. Thank goodness they *weren't* alike! But there was something about Janey's smile, her colouring and the way she walked. Something in her beauty now that she knew how to let it show.

Was he looking for Alice, then? Was there still some stubborn ghost of Luke's old attraction to his ex-wife lingering inside him? Was that why he wanted to keep watching this woman? Was that why he'd been so hungry to make love to her last night?

Janey was grieving for her sister, and he'd grieved, too, because his son had lost a mother. But he'd had so much anger towards Alice over the past five years. He wanted to let all of it go—the memory of his shallow infatuation, the sense of bitter betrayal, the agony of losing his child.

If his attraction to Janey came from a subconsious desire to find the best parts of Alice, then he didn't want it, not at all.

Let it go, he urged himself. Don't think about it. Don't feel it.

But then, watching Janey lift her hot dark hair to cool the skin at the back of her neck, he suddenly remembered the party she'd talked about last night.

Yes! That's right! He could picture her now! She'd been wearing a glittering silver dress, shimmying her hips, closing her eyes, dancing with a champagne glass in her hand. The room had been dark, the music and laughter deafening.

They'd all got hot and sweaty, and she'd lifted her hair up from her neck just like that, just the way she was doing now, and in his drunken state he'd had this hazy thought, Wow! She's all right when she lets herself go. She's beautiful. I knew she would be…

He still didn't remember the actual kiss. He'd been so exhausted that night he'd started seeing stars, but he remembered Janey, and what he'd thought about her.

It hit him in a blinding flash of understanding that he had been totally wrong. He wasn't looking for Alice in Janey. That wasn't why he'd wanted her so much last night, and wanted her still.

Never.

It was—and always had been—the other way around.

Eight years ago, when he'd first met Alice, the reason he'd fallen for her so hard and so fast and so disastrously had been because he'd subconsciously thought he was getting Janey's mind and spirit, her work ethic, her good sense and her grounded soul, all packaged in the instant, charismatic appeal of Alice's confidence and effervescence and beauty.

He'd been looking for Janey in Alice, and he'd been so, so wrong about both of them.

Oh, *hell*!

And then he understood something else—that now, though he had no right to expect or ask for it, he might— just *might*—have earned a second chance at getting things right. The way she'd responded to him last night. The looks she gave him sometimes, full of trust. The love she showed for his son, every minute.

'Behind you. She's going the other way, over,' he heard on the walkie-talkie. He hadn't been paying attention for the past few minutes. He'd been miles away, learning the truth about his heart. Learning too late? How much had he hurt her by making love to her and then not remembering their kiss? Why had she made such a point about something so messy and so long ago?

'I've got her, I can see her. No... She's gone into the undergrowth. It's so thick, I'm not keeping up, and I can't hear her.'

'Which direction? Over.'

'Can't tell.'

'I can see her!' Rowdy suddenly whispered. 'I see her! I see her! She's coming this way.'

'Yes!' Janey exclaimed. 'I think that's her. I saw a flash of blue.'

Luke fumbled for the control button on the walkie-talkie. 'This is Luke. Looks like we have her coming out into the clearing, over.'

'She's right here,' Rowdy said.

'Luke again.' He had to fight to concentrate. He was still thinking about Janey.

She'd stood up to watch the big, flightless bird picking its way into the open in search of the fruit it could smell. Her lithe, long-legged body was poised in electric concentration, with one foot on the ground and a knee resting on the bench. Her arm brushed Rowdy's little shoulder. The two of them were both riveted by what was happening, and Luke had a fresh understanding of how important this was.

They could still lose the bird, and what would that do to his son?

He spoke into the walkie-talkie. 'She's coming into the open, moving slowly. Limping. The leg looks nasty.'

He heard a crackling, and then Ben Chandler's voice. 'Stay quiet, OK? Is she going for the fruit?'

'Yes. She's just found it.'

'That gives us some time to get there.'

The minutes passed, slow and tight with tension. Elke grazed greedily on the squashy, colourful fruit. It was almost gone. Would she stay there, looking for more, or limp back into the undergrowth? She'd begun to nudge the ground with her beak, her keel-shaped crest bobbing up and down. She was getting impatient. The feast looked to be over.

Then they saw a flicker of movement, not the bright plumage of a rainforest bird but the more muted colours of Ben's gear. He wore a chest protector, chainsaw chaps and groin protector, and carried a pole injector—more or less a syringe and needle at the end of a six-foot pole, Luke had seen. Ben stopped at the edge of the undergrowth. Elke had sensed his presence. What would she do? Which way would she run? Or would the remaining fruit keep her where she was long enough? Rowdy was holding his breath.

Ben loped forward and pushed the pole into the bird, his movement so fast and quiet that Luke couldn't see which bit of the creature he'd hit. But apparently he'd got the dose into her because she teetered on her feet, stumbled a few paces and then fell.

'Is she OK?' Rowdy asked.

They'd told him about the sedating medication in the syringe, but Janey reassured him, 'She's gone to sleep, kind of. She'd be too scared and she wouldn't be safe to handle if she was awake, remember?'

'But she'll wake up again, won't she? She's not dead?'

'No, she's not dead, sweetheart. She's fine. She'll wake up later on.'

Ben came cautiously up to the bird, speaking into his walkie-talkie. 'Bring the buggy around,' they heard him say. Behind him petite, black-haired Julie Nguyen emerged with a tarpaulin and the two of them slid the limp bird onto it with a degree of effort. It must weigh fifty kilos or more, Luke thought.

'Can we go and see her?' Rowdy asked.

Luke waved at Ben who nodded. When they reached the centre of the clearing, Julie had begun to examine the bird. 'The leg's not broken, thank goodness. They're such difficult patients, they don't survive fractures. But, still, the muscle is badly torn. Not looking good. She'll need it cleaned and stitched, and she'll need antibiotics.' She had a broad Australian accent, a sweet voice and a cheerful manner. 'If she'd been a wild bird, I'm not sure if we could have pulled her through because the recovery period would stress her too much, but the fact that she was raised in captivity and will be in familiar surroundings should work in her favour. I think she'll be fine. We just need to get her back to the animal care room, where we can work on her before she wakes up.'

'So she's not going to die?' Rowdy said.

Had Julie been briefed? She bent down to him,

propping her hands on her knees. The silky black of her ponytail swung over her shoulder. 'She's not going to die.'

'You're not going to shoot her because she hurt Sam?'

'No, because she's going back in a really good cage so she won't be able to hurt anyone else. Thanks for helping us capture her. It wasn't safe to leave her in the wild. Hey, if she and Fred have some babies, want to think of some names for them? Send us an e-mail and tell us what you think they should be called.'

'Names!' He looked very seriously at Janey, a little overwhelmed by the new responsibility. He was exhausted, Luke realised.

'No hurry, Rowdy,' he said quickly. 'Think about it another day. I bet you can come up with some great names if you give it some thought. Can we grab a ride back to the resort in one of the buggies?' he asked Ben. 'We won't wait while you load Elke up. It's getting late.'

He put his arm around Janey without even thinking about it and squeezed her hard. She squeezed him back, but then drew away uncertainly and sneaked a look up into his face that she didn't want him to see. He didn't know what she felt, whether from her point of view there was anything more than his son bringing them close like this. There had to be, didn't there? What was she thinking about last night?

Despite his earth-shattering understanding of what had really been going on in his head and his heart eight years ago, he still felt on very shaky ground.

CHAPTER NINE

LUKE watched the day's last boat back to the mainland churning out into the open water, leaving a path of white wake that seemed to glow in the rapidly fading light. 'Look's like we're spending the night on the island. I'll have to call Charles so he can get someone to cover for me at the hospital tomorrow.'

'If we can get a cabin, it sounds like a nice idea, not a setback,' Janey told him. 'Rowdy's wiped out, and so am I.' She tucked a strand of hair behind her ear and pushed several more back from her forehead.

'We haven't asked him yet how he feels about being called Rowdy.'

'You think now's the time?'

'We should make sure, not just let it slide. Sometimes kids accept things because they don't realise it can be different, don't you think?' He walked over to his son, standing beside the dock rail, and bent down to him, knowing that Janey was just behind him, listening. He needed to do this right. 'Rowdy?'

'Are we staying the night?'

'Looks that way. But can I ask you something?'

Rowdy nodded.

'We've been calling you Rowdy. Do you like that, or do you want to be called something else?'

'You mean Felixx, or one of my other names?'

'Your other names?'

'Mum changed her mind. When I was four, she thought Nuriel was the right name. But then it didn't fit my spirit, she said, and she tried Rami, but that didn't fit either. I can't remember what my name was before Nuriel. Max and CJ call me Rowdy, and so does Georgie. I like it.'

'Know what?' Luke said, in a slightly unsteady voice. 'So do I!'

He stood up and circled back to Janey, spreading his hands in a silent question. She nodded, and he knew she approved. 'Now, let's organise that cabin,' she said, 'before I collapse in a screaming heap. I'm a wreck!'

'You look good.' While he felt sticky with sweat.

She laughed. 'Yeah, right!'

He didn't argue, just held her gaze for a little too long and left her to make of it what she wanted. She *did* look good. Sun-kissed skin on her cheeks and shoulders, the fresh evening breeze blowing her hair. A weary yet contented smile.

Some good things had happened today—new beginnings born from danger—and she had hope in her face now. For Rowdy. For herself.

For me?

He took a moment to think about the kind of beauty she had. An unusual kind. So responsive to how she felt inside. When she was down or stressed or doubting of herself, her face went tight and forbidding. But when she was happy, when she let herself fly, she totally glowed.

Yeah, Janey Stafford, no matter what you might think, you look good.

'We have an in with management—shall we use it?' he said. 'See if Andrew can wangle us something really nice?'

In the end they didn't have to lean on Andrew for any favours. The resort had had plenty of cancellations thanks to the cyclone, and there was a three-bedroom luxury cabin with private deck and Jacuzzi available. 'For you three, complimentary, with a four-course room-service dinner and wine thrown in,' Andrew told them.

'I think two courses is probably enough for this little guy,' Luke told him.

'What would you like, mate?'

'You eat pretty much everything, don't you, Rowdy?'

'I think hamburgers with everything are good,' he said seriously. 'And tropical juice. And cake with fruit salad and cream, like we had at lunch.'

'There you go, is that do-able?' Luke asked.

'No worries.'

'If we could have it pretty soon, because bedtime's not going to hold off much longer.' He looked at Janey for confirmation, and she nodded. 'But maybe save the four courses and wine until eight o'clock or so?' he finished.

'Whatever you want.'

Andrew summoned someone to show them their cabin, and Janey announced as soon as he had gone, 'I think I'm going to cry!'

'Why?'

'Because it's so clean and airy and nice, and I'm so tired, and so hungry I could eat about six of Rowdy's hamburgers.'

'Have a shower.' He looked at her more closely and saw that she was actually trembling, her blood sugar had dropped so low. 'And then a soak in the Jacuzzi on the deck. He's a self-feeding organism. I'll get him ready for bed.'

She gave him a suspicious look, and the air crackled with last night's tension suddenly. 'You're spoiling me. Do you think I'm about to collapse in a screaming heap or something? I've been out of hospital for two and a half days.'

'Yeah, and that's not long enough. As your doctor, I'm prescribing a shower and a hot tub.'

'You're not my doctor.'

'And you're too fond of a good argument.'

'Only this isn't a good one, because I'm too tired. You're right. I need the hot tub.'

It was sheer heaven. Janey washed off the sand and salt, shampooed her sweaty hair, then wrapped herself in a huge, fluffy towel, went out to the jacuzzi and was faced with a decision.

Put Georgie's salty swimsuit back on?

Really, it didn't quite fit her, and the straps had been digging into her shoulders all day. A wooden lattice screen made the hot tub very private, as did the churning foam covering the surface. No one would see...

So, not much of a decision, as it turned out.

She dropped the towel onto the wooden decking, lowered herself into the tub and floated there with her eyes closed while the tension drained from her body. The water churned, buffeting her tired muscles and coaxing all thought from her mind. She could easily have fallen asleep...

'Auntie Janey?'

Her eyes drifted open. Rowdy stood on the deck, leaning on the side of the hot tub so that a pair of big

brown eyes were just inches from her face. 'Hi, sweetheart,' she said. How long had she been in here? She
hadn't really intended to leave Luke to put him to bed.
'Was your hamburger good?' She knew he must have
eaten it, because there were beetroot stains and bun
crumbs and a tomato seed still on his face.

But Rowdy didn't have hamburgers on his mind any
more.

'Luke says he's my dad.' He almost had to yell the
words, over the churning sound of the hot-tub jets. 'Is he?'

Janey's heart went thump, and her sleepy content-
ment dropped from her like a stone.

Luke appeared, looming behind Rowdy, his eyes
narrowed. He raked his white teeth across his bottom
lip. 'It just came up,' he mouthed, over his son's head.
He took an agitated pace. 'I hadn't planned on...' He
stopped, looking helpless.

'Is he my dad?' Rowdy repeated. 'Mum never said.'

And, of course, Rowdy needed the truth now. He'd
had so much uncertainty and so much chaos in his little
life. He'd lost his mum. He needed the truth.

Janey took a deep breath and just said it. 'Yes, he is,
love.'

'Why? How is he my dad?' he yelled.

She reached for the button on the side of the tub that
turned off the jets. They couldn't *shout* this conversation.

'He and your mum were married,' she said. 'But
sometimes people discover that they can't be married
to each other after all, and they're not happy and they
fight, and that's not good if they have a child. So they
separate—move to different houses or different towns—
and the baby goes with either the mum or the dad.'

She came upon the issue of shared custody in her

head, examined it for a moment, and let it go. She had to make this as simple as possible, and about Rowdy himself, not about the myriad scenarios that could happen to kids after a divorce.

She stretched a wet, slippery arm out of the hot tub and took his hand. 'You went with your mum, and she lived in a couple of different places, but then she took you to Mundarri, and she decided not to tell you that you had a dad, because he was too far away.'

He nodded. 'In Crocodile Creek.'

Which seemed far away to him. Janey looked at London, looked at Alice concealing her whereabouts from Luke for so long, and let that go, too.

'When she died, I brought you to Crocodile Creek so we could meet your dad, but then we had the bus accident, and everything got complicated and Luke and I talked about it and decided to wait a while before we told you who he was. But then...' She trailed off. Luke would have to pick up the story now.

He came forward and sat on the edge of the jacuzzi. 'But then we were talking just now, you and me, and you asked a couple of questions, and I don't like telling lies. I thought you'd want to hear the truth. Is it OK, Rowdy?'

Out of his son's range of vision, he rolled his eyes and pressed his palm to his forehead. *I'm stuffing this up.*

Janey shook her head. *You're not.*

'I'd like to have a dad,' Rowdy said cautiously. 'Do I have to live at your house, with all the doctors?'

'You don't have to, but we—'

'I want to live with Auntie Janey.'

'Do you? I guess you would. She's pretty good, isn't she?'

'Yes.'

'I think so, too.' There was a tiny pause. Luke seemed to be thinking fast, weighing up options Janey couldn't quite read. 'Here's a plan, then. Janey, stop me straight away if I'm going too fast.' It sounded like a warning.

'Too fast?'

'Although it feels to me, right now, as if I'm eight years too slow.'

That, she couldn't answer. She met Luke's gaze once more, over the top of Rowdy's head. She couldn't breathe. Something hung in the air, a moment so important and pivotal she didn't have a name for it, or a word for how she felt. What could she say? Eight years too *slow*? Eight *years*?

Luke spoke. 'I want to live with Auntie Janey, too,' he said, not taking his eyes from her face for a second.

What was he doing? Rowdy looked between the two of them, up over his shoulder at Luke, down at Janey, with the deck's yellow lighting gleaming on the water. He was confused, and waiting for more.

So am I.

'Luke?' she whispered.

'I want to marry her, and then the three of us can live together.'

'In Crocodile Creek?' Rowdy asked.

'If you want. If she wants. Janey?'

'Marry you?' Her heart began to beat faster.

'Yes.'

'Because...?' *Of Rowdy?*

He understood at once. 'No, not because. For a million other reasons. For the one reason that really counts. Tell me, Janey, so I know if we're on the right track here.'

'I think we're on the right track,' she said faintly.

'Just think?'

'I—I have questions.'

'Which I can answer.' He leaned closer. 'You see, Rowdy, I knew her before I met your mum, and we were always friends. Sometimes we didn't quite understand that we were friends, because we got annoyed with each other a lot. People make mistakes about how they feel sometimes. There was so much I didn't understand then…'

Who is he really talking to? Rowdy or me? Himself?

'But I'm not making a mistake about Auntie Janey now. She reminded me about something last night. A party we went to once. And I didn't remember while she was telling me about it, but today in the bird hide it suddenly came back to me. And I realized…' He stopped. 'But that's for Auntie Janey and me to talk about later. Janey?'

'Yes. It's insane. It's not,' she corrected quickly. 'It feels insane. But when I think… I'm not sounding sensible, am I?'

He sat on the edge of the hot tub. 'Not very. We're waiting for a clear answer, Rowdy and I.'

And she knew that Rowdy needed one.

'Luke and I are going to get married, Rowdy,' she said, and as soon as the words were spoken, clear and plain, the way he needed, they sounded right.

'Well, he's asleep already,' Luke said ten minutes later, coming out of the bedroom Rowdy had chosen for himself. 'So I guess he's OK with everything for the moment.' He paused, then spoke quietly. 'Are you OK with it, Janey? I sprang it on you. It wasn't the right time. I didn't know what else to do. Can we make it the right time now? I love you. Can't even say it in words.'

He covered the remaining space between them in three paces. 'Will you marry me, sweetheart?'

'Oh, Luke…' She reached out her arms and whispered, 'Do I really need to tell you?'

She pressed her cheek against his, smelling the clean scent of his recent shower on his warm skin. They were both wrapped in the resort's tropical kimono-style robes. 'Tell me anyway,' he whispered, seeking her mouth.

'I love you. I'll marry you.'

He kissed her with deep, sweet, hungry heat. They grinned at each other, stroked each other's hair, kissed again even more deeply, and then he just held her, and it was all she wanted. 'At first I kept feeling Alice's ghost…' he said.

'Me, too.'

'Not real, but in my head.'

'I know.'

'I'd been so angry with her, but I still couldn't help wondering.'

'If you were looking for her when you looked at me?'

'Yes. And then in the hide today it hit me. I was never looking for her in you. It was the other way around. Always. Eight years ago, when you used to drive me so crazy and we'd rub each other up the wrong way, have those arguments while we washed the dishes at your parents' place at Christmas and birthday gatherings, or in groups of doctors at work. It was only because I wanted you.'

'Wanted *me*?'

'I think you wanted me, too.'

'Only I wasn't ready. Plus you were too perfect, and you knew it.'

'And you were impossible. And that was what drove me so crazy, that you didn't have the first idea of how much you were worth. A lot more than I had to give you at that point in my life, to be honest.'

'No…'

'Yes. Now I'll give you my whole heart, and it's bigger than it used to be.'

'We've both grown up…'

'Janey, I was looking for you in Alice, and I was so blind to think I could have found all of your qualities in her.'

'You remembered the kiss.'

'I remembered you in a silver dress. Did you ever wear that again?'

'I borrowed it. It was an act of madness, not my kind of thing at all. Sent all the wrong signals, I thought.'

'You looked fabulous. The way you danced. The way you smiled. The way you let your hair fall all over your face and just went wild. And in the hide I remembered this smug moment of thinking at the party that I'd known all along that you could be fabulous, and that was when I realised the truth. And it means we can let Alice go.'

'Let her go?'

'She'll always be your sister, and Rowdy's mother, but she's not and never has been the woman I'm searching for, with you as her substitute. You have to know that, Janey. It's always been you.'

'And it always will be you, Luke, in my heart,' she promised him in a whisper as she looked into his amber eyes. 'For the rest of my life.'

On the beach at Crocodile Creek, in the cove below the Athina Hotel, a bonfire blazed while the sun began to set behind the cyclone-ravaged mountains to the west. The debris from the cyclone had been piled in several heaps off to the side of tonight's gathering, gentle waves had deposited much of the churned-up sand back onto the beach, and in the fading light you couldn't even see the damage, only the beauty.

Luke, Janey and Rowdy had caught the five o'clock boat back from Charm Island, a day later than originally planned, and had driven straight to the cove from the boat dock in Crocodile Creek's tiny harbour. Cal and Gina's wedding ceremony was scheduled to begin at six o'clock.

Most people had already gathered when they came down towards the water, but there were still some late arrivals streaming ahead of them onto the sand, carrying eskies or baskets or foil-covered dishes. The Grubbs' way of catering for the event had been to get everyone to bring a contribution.

Janey saw several smoking pits of coals in the sand, and there seemed to be a massive array of food, either already baking or waiting to go in. She saw pineapples and prawns and whole fish, two dozen parcels of something wrapped in fresh banana leaves, cubes of chicken and meat on bamboo skewers, piles of marshmallows and pots of chocolate sauce, salads and cakes and wine.

She recognised Georgie and Alistair—the latter gave Georgie's backside a lascivious pat as she watched—and Christina and Joe. Christina sat in a wheelchair that looked somewhat bogged down in the sand, and she had baby Isabella in her arms. There was Mrs Grubb and her husband Walter, Max and CJ, Charles and Jill and little Lily. She found faces that she couldn't put a name to yet as well, but could make guesses about.

Those two pretty blondes had to be Susie and Hannah Jackson, because she didn't think Crocodile Creek had two pairs of identical medical twins. And the twin with her arms around a good-looking man had to be Hannah, because the man would be Ryan Fisher, her new fiancé. They were returning to New Zealand early next week, she thought.

The slightly plump and freckled but beaming woman standing next to a uniformed police officer was Grace O'Riordan, whom she'd only met briefly, and the officer was Harry Blake. That was the groom, Cal, standing with a couple of mates, near a woman who must be the marriage celebrant. He had bare feet and wore white gabardine jeans and a tropical patterned shirt in white and silver-grey. She realised that CJ was dressed the same way. Several cameras clicked, and everyone looked nervous, including the two groomsmen, but what were their names?

My head's starting to hurt!

Janey gave up her attempt to identify everyone. She'd get to know them soon enough. She was staying in Crocodile Creek. Rowdy ran down the beach and spotted Max and CJ, who were doing long jumps in the sand, vying for the most impressive style and the most wildly scissoring legs. 'Hey, guys, watch this!' he yelled, and launched into the air, windmilling his arms and landing in a messy heap.

'No, watch *this*!' yelled Max, immediately determined to outdo a mere five-year-old. He didn't bat an eyelid at the fact that Rowdy had spoken, and neither did CJ.

But several of the adults turned to Janey and Luke, surprised, questioning, pleased. Georgie gave a thumbs-up sign. She was grinning her head off.

'We worked a couple of things out,' Luke said. He

glanced up to the path leading down to the beach. 'Tell you later.'

Because here was the bride, wearing silver thongs and a white slip dress shimmering with beads. She had white flowers in her hair. She waved at CJ and he hurried to take his place beside Cal.

'I can do an even bigger one!' Rowdy yelled to Max.

'Listen to him,' Luke said softly.

'I know,' Janey whispered back. 'It's wonderful.'

They stepped close to each other, he put his arm around her and she leaned against him, belonging there with every cell in her body. A beach wedding might be really nice, Janey decided, when it was their own turn...

'Looks like you worked out a heck of a lot,' said Georgie.

'All the important stuff,' Luke answered. 'We still have to refine a few details.'

'Are you staying in Crocodile Creek?'

'What can I do? Janey loves a bit of heat.' He slid his hand down to her hip and she turned her face up for a kiss.

'Whew, you don't have to tell me. I can feel it from here,' Georgie said, fanning herself.

Gina arrived at Cal's side, everyone fell silent—even Rowdy—and their simple ceremony began, with the waves lapping on the beach and a certain happy realisation in the air that there would be more weddings in Crocodile Creek before too long.

BRIDES OF PENHALLY BAY

Medical™ is proud to welcome you to Penhally
Bay Surgery where you can meet the team led by
caring and commanding Dr Nick Tremayne.
For twelve months we will bring you an
emotional, tempting romance – devoted
doctors, single fathers, a sheikh surgeon,
royalty, blushing brides and miracle babies
that will warm your heart…

*Let us whisk you away to this Cornish coastal
town – to a place where hearts are made whole.*

Turn the page for a sneak preview from
The Italian's New Year Marriage Wish
by Sarah Morgan
– the second book in the
BRIDES OF PENHALLY BAY series.

THE ITALIAN'S NEW YEAR
MARRIAGE WISH
by
Sarah Morgan

'*Sì*, come in.'

The sound of his smooth, confident voice made her stomach lurch and she closed her eyes briefly. Despite his enviable fluency in English, no one could ever have mistaken Marco Avanti for anything other than an Italian and his voice stroked her nerve endings like a caress.

Her palm was damp with nerves as she clutched the door-handle and turned it.

He was just a man like any other.

She wasn't going to go weak at the knees. She wasn't going to notice anything about him. She was past all that. She was just going to say what needed to be said and then leave.

Ten minutes, she reminded herself. She just had to survive ten minutes and not back down. And then she'd be on the train back to London.

She opened the door and stepped into the room. 'Hello, Marco.' Her heart fluttered like the wings of a captive butterfly as she forced herself to look at him. 'I wanted to have a quick word before you start surgery.'

His dark eyes met hers and heat erupted through her body, swift and deadly as a forest fire. From throat to pelvis she burned, her reaction to him as powerful as ever. Helplessly, she dug her fingers into her palms.

A man like any other? Had she really believed that, even for a moment? Marco was nothing like any other man.

She'd had two years to prepare herself for this moment, so why did the sight of him drive the last of her breath from her body? What was it about him? Yes, he was handsome but other men were handsome and she barely noticed them. Marco was different. Marco was the embodiment of everything it was to be male. He was strong, confident and unashamedly macho and no woman with a pulse could look at him and not want him.

And for a while he'd been hers.

She looked at him now, unable to think of anything but the hungry, all-consuming passion that had devoured them both.

His powerful body was ominously still, but he said nothing. He simply leaned slowly back in his chair and watched her in brooding silence, his long fingers toying with the pen that he'd been using when she'd entered the room.

Desperately unsettled, Amy sensed the slow simmer of emotion that lay beneath his neutral expression.

What wouldn't she have given to possess even a tiny fraction of his cool?

'We need to talk to each other.' She stayed in the doorway, her hands clasped nervously in front of her, a shiver passing through her body as the atmosphere in the room suddenly turned icy cold.

Finally he spoke. 'You have chosen an odd time of day for a reunion.'

'This isn't a reunion. We have things to discuss, you know we do.'

His gaze didn't flicker. 'And I have thirty sick patients to see before lunchtime. You shouldn't need to ask where my priorities lie.'

No, she didn't need to ask. His skill and dedication as a doctor was one of the qualities that had attracted her to him in the first place.

His handsome face was hard and unforgiving and she felt her insides sink with misery.

What had she expected?

He was hardly going to greet her warmly, was he? Not after the way she'd treated him. *Not after the things she'd let him think about her.* 'I didn't have any choice but to come and see you, Marco. You didn't answer my letters.'

'I didn't like the subject matter.' There was no missing the hard edge to his tone. 'Write about something that interests me and I'll consider replying. And now you need to leave because my first patient is waiting.'

'No.' Panic slid through her and she took a little step forward. 'We need to do this. I know you're upset, but—'

'*Upset?*' One dark eyebrow rose in sardonic appraisal. 'Why would you possibly think that?'

Her breathing was rapid. 'Please, don't play games—it isn't going to help either of us. Yes, I left, but it was the right thing to do, Marco. It was the right thing for both of us. I'm sure you can understand that now that some time has passed.'

'I understand that you walked out on our marriage. You think "upset"...' his accent thickened as he lingered on the word. 'You think "upset" is an accurate description of my feelings on this subject?'

Amy felt the colour touch her cheeks. The truth was that she had absolutely no insight into his feelings. She'd never really known what he had truly been feeling at any point in their relationship and she hadn't been around to witness his reaction to her departure. If he had been upset then she assumed that it would have been because she'd exposed him to the gossip of a small community, or possibly because he'd had a life plan and she'd ruined it. Not because he'd loved her, because she knew that had never been the case. How could he have loved her? What had she ever been able to offer a man like Marco Avanti?

Especially not once she'd discovered—

Unable to cope with that particular thought at the moment, Amy lifted her chin and ploughed on. 'I can see that you're angry and I don't blame you, but I didn't come here to argue. We can make this easy or we can make it difficult.'

'And I'm sure you're choosing easy.' The contempt in his tone stung like vinegar on an open wound. 'You chose to walk away rather than sort out a problem. Isn't that what you're good at?'

'Not every problem has a solution, Marco!' Frustrated and realising that if she wasn't careful she risked revealing more than she wanted to reveal, she moved closer to the desk. 'You have every right to be upset, but what we need now is to sort out the future. I just need you to agree to the divorce. Then you'll be free to…' *Marry another woman?* The words stuck in her throat.

'*Accidenti*, am I right in understanding that you have interrupted my morning surgery to *ask me for a divorce*?' He rose to his feet, his temper bubbling to the surface, a dangerous glint in his molten dark eyes. 'It is bad enough that I am expected to diagnose a multitude of potentially serious illnesses in a five-minute consultation, but now my wife decides that that in that same ridiculous time frame we are going to end our relationship. This is your idea of a joke, no?'

She'd forgotten how tall he was, how imposing. He topped six feet two and his shoulders were broad and powerful. Looking at him now, she had to force herself not to retreat to the safety of Reception. 'It's not a joke and if I'm interrupting your surgery, it's your fault. You wouldn't answer my letters. I had no other way of getting in touch with you. And this needn't take long.'

He gripped the edge of the desk and his knuckles whitened. 'Do you really think you can leave without explanation and then walk back in here and end our marriage with a five-minute conversation?' His eyes blazed with anger and his voice rose. *'Is that what you think?'*

Startled by his unexpected loss of control, Amy flinched. *She hadn't thought he'd cared so much.*

FREE!

4 Books
and a surprise gift!

We would like to take this opportunity to thank you for reading this Mills & Boon® book by offering you the chance to take FOUR more specially selected titles from the Medical™ series absolutely FREE! We're also making this offer to introduce you to the benefits of the Mills & Boon® Reader Service™—

- ★ **FREE home delivery**
- ★ **FREE gifts and competitions**
- ★ **FREE monthly Newsletter**
- ★ **Exclusive Reader Service offers**
- ★ **Books available before they're in the shops**

Accepting these FREE books and gift places you under no obligation to buy, you may cancel at any time, even after receiving your free shipment. Simply complete your details below and return the entire page to the address below. You don't even need a stamp!

YES! Please send me 4 free Medical books and a surprise gift. I understand that unless you hear from me, I will receive 6 superb new titles every month for just £2.89 each, postage and packing free. I am under no obligation to purchase any books and may cancel my subscription at any time. The free books and gift will be mine to keep in any case.

M7ZEF

Ms/Mrs/Miss/Mr .... Initials ....
BLOCK CAPITALS PLEASE
Surname ....
Address ....

....

.... Postcode ....

Send this whole page to:
UK: FREEPOST CN81, Croydon, CR9 3WZ